LIVE FOR TODAY

TONY IRWIN

Grosvenor House
Publishing Limited

All rights reserved
Copyright © Tony Irwin, 2023

The right of Tony Irwin to be identified as the author of this
work has been asserted in accordance with Section 78
of the Copyright, Designs and Patents Act 1988

The book cover is copyright to Tony Irwin

This book is published by
Grosvenor House Publishing Ltd
Link House
140 The Broadway, Tolworth, Surrey, KT6 7HT.
www.grosvenorhousepublishing.co.uk

This book is sold subject to the conditions that it shall not, by way of
trade or otherwise, be lent, resold, hired out or otherwise circulated
without the author's or publisher's prior consent in any form of
binding or cover other than that in which it is published and
without a similar condition including this condition being
imposed on the subsequent purchaser.

This book is a work of fiction. Any resemblance to
people or events, past or present, is purely coincidental.

A CIP record for this book
is available from the British Library

ISBN 978-1-80381-706-4
eBook ISBN 978-1-80381-707-1

Dedications

This book is dedicated to the heroes who risk their lives to help others in war zones and take exceptional risks for no financial reward or kudos.

I would also like to thank my friend and author from across the pond, Marcia Kellam, for her unwavering support and advice.

And most of all, to my wife Jean for her steadfast encouragement and help.

Preface

This is a prequel to my first novel, *Don't Stop for Anything*. It traces the life of two characters who remained in Syria during the civil war to help the best they could.

He who finds calamity in others finds his own calamity light.
An Arabic proverb, source unknown.

Table of Contents

Part 1 Ali's Story 1

    Chapter 1 Raqqa Prison, 2014 3

    Chapter 2 Oxford England, 1994 4

    Chapter 3 Detective Work 41

    Chapter 4 The Syria Trip, 1995 49

    Chapter 5 Back at Oxford, 1995 69

    Chapter 6 Antalya Ali Recovering, 2014 77

    Chapter 7 Moving to Syria, 1996 90

    Chapter 8 Allan James, 1996 99

    Chapter 9 The Trial, 1996 109

    Chapter 10 Civil Unrest 119

    Chapter 11 Raqqa Prison, 2014 131

    Chapter 12 UK, 2014 135

Part 2 Margaret's Story 143

    Chapter 13 1994 145

    Chapter 14 The Destruction of Aleppo, 2013 155

    Chapter 15 Nursing Ali 173

    Chapter 16 Back in the UK 178

    Chapter 17 With Baba at Last. 199

    Chapter 18 The Letters 215

    Chapter 19 Hua 223

    Chapter 20 Pembrokeshire 240

    Chapter 21 Fatima 246

    Chapter 22 Christmas, 2015 250

    Chapter 23 Back at Frimley Hospital 253

    Chapter 24 Bad News 257

    Chapter 25 Life Without Ali 261

Part 1
Ali's Story

Chapter 1

Raqqa Prison, 2014

Curled naked on a filthy, cold, stinking hammam floor, my fight for survival is over. No pain, thirst, hunger, at last contentment.

No more beatings?
What happens next?
Endless sleep?
Nothing?

Solid arms cradling me.

Am I being lifted and carried?
Floating maybe?
My spirit leaving my body?
So, this is death?
Am I on my way to the other place?
Is there such a thing?
Was I wrong?
There is life after death?

Chapter 2
Oxford England, 1994

According to the estate agent, my second-floor apartment was in a house of multiple occupation. Consisting of four floors, each floor contained an apartment with two private bedrooms, a shared bathroom, and a kitchen connected by a hall leading to the entrance door. A staircase connected each floor with an entry door into what the agent called a shared self-contained flat. My bedroom had a large bed, a wardrobe, and a table with two chairs. The Oxford Syrian Society insisted it would be ideal for me, being more private than most student accommodations. It was desirable because it was Georgian, *whatever that meant*.

My father was concerned about me living and mixing with non-believers in a non-Muslim country. So, I promised to obey him, join a mosque as soon as possible, and continue praying five times daily. He also warned me that Christians would attempt to convert me to their religion and their sinful ways.

He lectured, "It is their way; remember the Crusaders and what they did to us. They will try to convert you, not by the sword this time, but by derogating the teachings of Allah."

I had preconceived ideas of life in England gathered from television, films, hearsay, propaganda, and my father. So, I was unsurprised to find that men and women mixed openly, even if not family members. What was a shock was how freely they showed affection towards each other. Holding hands in public, embracing, and sometimes kissing, not on each cheek, but on the mouth. Being accustomed to women walking behind men and never touching each other made me incredibly uneasy. Women dressed in clothes that reveal their feminine shape, hair uncovered, and flesh meant only for a husband's eyes troubled me. It went against all my teachings.

I shared the flat with another student called George Newall. To begin with, I didn't see much of George as we kept well to ourselves. I presumed George, like me, was coming to terms with studying and had little time for anything else. The shared kitchen wasn't an issue for me as an Arab, as we are raised to share. It's the polite thing to do. It was clear George didn't have the same values as me. I would often find the fridge and cupboards empty of food. I always bought ample for two people. So, hungry and finding the cupboards bare, annoyed, I knocked on George's bedroom door to see if the issue could be resolved.

I had only seen George fleetingly. I observed he was tall, thin, and white-skinned with a mop of unkempt blonde curly hair, always wearing the same creased shirt, torn jeans, and grubby trainers. George opened the door, naked except for a purple sheet held around his skinny waist. *A strange colour.* He wedged the door ajar with his foot, leaning with his hand on the door frame – to perhaps obscure what was behind him?

Besides being almost naked, I also noticed a smell of incense and a glow from the bright red walls flickering behind him. *Candles, maybe?* George staggered a little. *Not fully awake?* His eyes were not fully open. *Adjusting to the hallway light?* Avoiding contact with mine.

He mumbled tetchily, "What does yer want?"

I felt a little embarrassed waking him up, but it was afternoon. So, in an apologetic tone, looking away from the door opening, I said. "Sorry for disturbing you. Can we talk about disappearing food?"

"Oh, that thing, sorted, okay?"

A female voice from inside the room called out, "George, tell him to piss off."

George waved his hand towards the voice. He repeated, "Sorted," and swiftly closed the door.

I wasn't enthusiastic that George took on board my complaint. So, I was surprised that the kitchen was replenished with food the following day. On the kitchen worktop was a scrawled note: 'I'm cooking tonight, George.'

Hearing activity in the kitchen – *George doing as he promised?* – I asked if I could help.

He replied, "Hell no, the treat is on me." Holding out his hand for me to shake. I gripped his hand firmly and shook it as most men do. His feeble hand collapsed. *Unused to physical work?* I released my grip in fear of hurting him.

"Ali Mansour."

"George Newall," he replied, staring directly into my eyes for a few seconds. *Judging me?*

"Can I be of any help?"

"No, the treat is on me; sit down. It won't take long."

"You sure?"

"You could crack open a couple of beers." I opened a can of beer and coke and placed two glasses on the table. "You, a Muslim?"

"Sorry, is that a problem?"

"No, not for me. It's your life."

George presented his meal on the table in two separate dishes, announcing, "My speciality, spag bol. There's plenty more, help yourself." He pointed to two saucepans on top of the range and a dish of grated parmesan cheese on the worktop.

During the meal, I learned George studied psychology and had plenty of free time. He took time when asking me personal questions and looked thoughtful before jumping to the next one. *Practising psychology, maybe?*

We talked over lots of things until the early hours. Possibly because we were so different in many ways. On parting, I told George the next meal was on me, and he replied, "Looking forward to it."

This started the unlikely friendship between two people with entirely different values. Precisely the type of person my father wanted me to avoid.

I gathered from George not all I was told about the sinful non-believers was true. Despite our differences, George was a gentle, thoughtful, kind man and always interested in my point of view. Though I could see he often disagreed with it. His values were different from mine, which I was about to fully understand after I cooked our first meal.

I prepared a typical Arabian dish of lamb and rice to be authentic. It should have been a Halal-slaughtered goat instead of a joint of lamb. *Were my Muslim values slipping already?* It should also have been eaten on the floor and served on a kabsa platter. The kitchen floor was too cramped and dirty and without the comfort of cushions. The kitchen table and a serving tray would have to do.

Nothing else was on the table except for the tray of food, a beer, and a coke. I explained to George the Arabic method of eating without utensils. Using the right hand only. I told George that clean hands were essential, and we both washed our hands in the kitchen sink. We sat in front of an impressive amount of food because the quality of a feast is measured by the quantity of food left uneaten.

I thought George would learn more about me, being a foreigner. Instead, I would learn more about myself as we ate the traditional Arab way, tearing the meat placed on a mountain of rice laced with herbs with our bare hands. I instructed George to only use his right hand to mix the rice and lamb and carefully pop the formed torpedo into his mouth.

George asked, smiling, "Why?"

I told him, "Satan eats and drinks with his left hand."

George had a mischievous look, which I would later get to know as 'taking the piss', as he called it. He then spouted, "I thought it was to do with wiping your arse with your left hand."

I showed my displeasure before replying, "We do not say such things when we eat the bounty God provided." I tried not to look too indignant.

Looking bemused, George said, "Hell, there's a little devil in all of us, but I won't upset your God."

He found eating the Arab way difficult but soon became adept and copied me. When I saw a choice piece of meat. I placed it before George to eat, and George copied me. "Knocks the socks off my spag bol. We, meaning you, must do this more often," George said with an appreciative smile. "Am I supposed to belch to prove the meal was good?"

"No, George, you are not supposed to."

George started a conversation regarding the different customs of sharing food. He explained it was a subject that was part of his thesis on culture. George pontificated, "Most nationalities have different traditions, but communal feasts are the norm for celebrations in most countries."

"In Syria, we always eat together, even with friends. We always share; we sit together at home, work, or school. I observed a group of workers taking a lunch break on a building site in Oxford. They sat in isolation, some distance apart, each with their lunchboxes. Muslim workers would have formed a circle around a cloth and placed their food between them to share equally, ensuring that the best food is given to one another. Do you think that's a more pleasant way of eating?"

"Communism works with small groups of people that trust each other."

"Communism – I wasn't talking about that."

"Commune-ism, with a hyphen, has been known to work on a small scale, fine in theory, but never lasts long in practice."

"George, in my Country, we share food with family, friends, visitors and everyone. We feel happy afterwards; that's not commune-ism, whichever way you say it. We are good Muslims."

"Okay, Ali, let us expand your theory of sharing. Would your president invite you to his feast? Give you the best bits. Is he a good Muslim?"

"Yes, he is, but I wouldn't expect him to invite the likes of me."

"Ali, we are all born human beings. According to most religions, we are all equal in the eyes of God. So why should we be unequal on earth?"

"That's the way of things."

"Don't you think it's convenient for those in power to punish coveting their wealth as a sin?"

"They have been chosen to rule over us."

"By whom?"

I remembered what my father told me about the Crusaders, so showing I was annoyed, I replied tersely, "By Allah, of course."

"No, Ali, they chose themselves." I didn't reply but shook my head from side to side vigorously in disagreement. "Ali, let us go back to the feast. Instead of food placed to share, imagine it was the wealth of everyone put on the table to share? How would it work? Those with little put all they have on the table. The wealthy put the least in proportion to their wealth. The rich are the only ones who gain when it's shared."

Later, I thought about the wealth of the heads of religions. The palaces they lived in and how isolated they were from the lives of ordinary people like me. Did George have a point?

George and I often shared meals, but we never discussed religion again. George clarified that he had three topics that were never open for discussion: sex, religion, and politics. George was an immense help in my studies, particularly the English language. When I needed help, he always had time for me. But George wouldn't help in modern warfare or anything military. George was a pacifist and insisted warfare was another no-go topic. I realised my father's concerns about people trying to convert me to their faith would not be an issue. As far as I could tell, most people had no religion and those that did paid little heed to it.

I acquired from George the wisdom to listen to another's point of view and consider their opinion. Never dismiss things you don't fully understand; first, listen to their argument, and then you might learn something. I was educated to ignore everything if it didn't fit the ideology of my faith or was told to me by my elders. I discovered the art of listening and discussing without getting excited if I couldn't win the debate. George was always calm and listened to my side before mostly disagreeing. Sometime later, he would cleverly use my contention to win an argument and convince me he was incorrect before. Always ending with, "It's open for discussion."

I noticed the comings and goings of girls who stayed overnight with George. I never got accustomed to accidentally bumping into them in the kitchen. The bathroom was often occupied for lengthy periods and smelt of perfume. I was always embarrassed as they were sparsely clad, though they never were. Sometimes, they were naked except for bath towels wrapped around their bodies that defied gravity. How they got them to stay in place, except for the corners tucked in, baffled me. *Why aren't they scared it would slip down?* They enjoyed the startled look on my face when I saw them almost naked as they nonchalantly passed me in the corridor with an accentuated wiggle.

George knocked on my bedroom door one evening. On opening it, he exclaimed, "Come on, enough studying. We are going out."

"Out? Where?"

"There's a quiz in the pub around the corner."

A bit dazed from studying, I replied, trying to sound not too uninterested, "Quiz? I have never been to one."

"That's an excellent argument to come then. You won't be able to use that excuse again."

"Pubs, sell alcohol."

"And coke. Get your coat; I need your brain."

Reluctantly, I agreed and was escorted to the pub. George seemed incredibly happy and placed an arm on my shoulder in a friendly manner. *Or to stop me from escaping?*

When we entered the pub, I didn't realise this was a life-changing moment. I didn't know what to expect: alcohol, men and women mixing freely? My father's warnings echoed, inducing a feeling of panic and reluctance combined with inquisitiveness.

The space inside the pub seemed to me bigger than outside. The room we entered was furnished with circular wooden tables with four chairs at each, not exactly matching each other. There were nooks and crannies, so seeing everyone in the room wasn't easy. The lighting didn't help; wall lights dimly lit produced a warm orange glow in small alcoves. We walked towards the table George had selected. "Hiya, George," was exclaimed as we passed small gatherings. People were talking over each other, producing a cacophony of noise.

Someone shouted, "Giving women a rest tonight, George?"

George bought a beer and a coke from the bar. Several young men came over, and he introduced me to them. I noticed a few female faces in the room from my embarrassing encounters in the flat. None of them looked in George's direction; I thought they would as he was well acquainted with them.

George explained how the quiz worked. "The questions are read out, and we have a few minutes to answer; if you know the answer, whisper it to me. Cup your hand so no one can hear or lip-read, okay? I'll write down the answers." On top of the answer paper was a space for a team name. "What should we call ourselves, Ali?"

"George and Ali."

"Bloody hell, have an imagination! Something cryptic, funny or clever."

"What about 'The Sorcerer's Apprentice'? Yes, that will do," George uttered, answering his own question.

"What's a sorcerer?"

"Wizard. You're a wizard, and I am your apprentice."

The quiz master gained attention by ringing a bell and shouting, "Let's be having yer!"

Immediately, the room fell to silence. The questions were read out and repeated after a pause. Though not always confident, I gave my answer to George, and he wrote something on the answer paper. When all the answer papers were completed, they were collected and redistributed to other teams to check and score.

George went to the bar and bought us both a drink. As he placed them on the table, he said, "The next round is yours."

"Round?"

"Turn."

Reluctantly, I replied, "Okay, George."

After quite a long wait, I asked George, looking at the time on my wristwatch, "When will the results be read out?"

"Some time yet, the landlord isn't daft. He'll keep everyone here drinking as long as possible. A quiz is a good earner; it brings the punters in." As the marked papers were collected, George said, "Round."

Apprehensively, on my way to the bar, I noticed a couple of young ladies, one with jet black and one with blonde hair. They smiled as I passed them, and I smiled back sheepishly. Eventually, the answers were read out. I was embarrassed as most of what I whispered to George was incorrect. We sat at the table, waiting for the team scores to be announced. "Sorry, George, this is going to be embarrassing."

The landlord rang a bell and announced, "In third place, 'Black and Blonde'. Second place, 'Two Blues'. The winners in first place with, wait for it, a perfect score, 'The Sorcerer's Apprentice'. A bottle of red wine goes to the winners."

I looked at George in amazement; *he hadn't listened to my answers.*

George knowingly grinned back at me, raised his hand and shouted to the landlord, "Over here!"

Black and Blonde were looking towards our table and smiling. George waved them over; the Blonde looked keen, but Black seemed reluctant.

Eventually, they came over. Blonde picked four wine glasses on the way. Blonde sat next to George, and Black reluctantly opposite me. Blonde introduced herself as Kirstie and coaxed Black to say Margaret.

Kirstie inquisitively asked, "Which one of you is the sorcerer?"

We pointed at each other.

Margaret looked at me. "You must be the bright one."

"Not me." I shook my head in denial.

She replied, "The modest ones are always the brightest."

"No, it's George," I replied earnestly.

Margaret replied, "You told George all the answers; I watched you."

George looked at me and smiled, saying, "He is an absolute wizard."

"That's settled," Kirstie announced with her finger on the cap of the wine bottle. Suggesting to George that it should be opened.

George smiled at Kirstie. "Be my guest."

Kirstie, holding the bottle, removed the cap. *How did she make it look provocative?* I could see a connection between George and Kirstie; they smiled like old friends. Then, they moved so that they were touching each other. Kirstie filled the four glasses of wine and passed one to each of us.

I shook my head. "Not for me, thank you."

"You can drink now, brainbox; the quiz is over. Losing a few brain cells will do no harm," Margaret said knowingly.

I looked at George for help, repeatedly moving my eyes to the glass in front of me and his eyes. He did the same to me, nodding and shrugging his shoulders, indicating it was my choice.

Kirstie raised her glass into the middle of the table, declaring, "To the winners, the spoils." Her eyes were fixed on George.

George and Margaret's glass clunked against Kirstie's. I felt compelled to join them and clunked my glass with their three. Almost in unison, they said, "Cheers!"

A millisecond later, I added, "Cheers."

They raised their glasses and took a sip. *What harm would it do just this once?* The taste of the wine wasn't pleasant. I copied the other three and sipped my wine as they did. I felt less embarrassed and more talkative as the wine lost its bitterness. I can't remember the conversation as I was not fully engaged. *What am I doing drinking alcohol in a pub?*

At the end of the evening, which George called 'throwing out time', George offered, "My place for a nightcap, anyone?"

Margaret replied without hesitation, "Count me out."

Kirstie, smiling, looked at George and said, "Okay, love too."

I could sense something was happening between George and Kirstie. *So this is what they meant by attraction.* I wasn't sure what a nightcap meant, but it brought George and Kirstie together as they walked to our flat with their arms around each other. Margaret walked beside me as we witnessed the couple in front getting more friendly. At the first corner, Margaret wished everyone goodnight. She walked away, waving her hand, leaving me behind the happy couple whispering and laughing. I didn't get a nightcap that night as George and Kirstie were impatient to get to his room.

I continued skipping with a rope daily to keep myself fit, which I had done since childhood. I wondered if there was a local skipping club, so I checked the university noticeboard. There was no skipping club but a swimming one with sessions for beginners. I hadn't learnt to swim correctly, so why not try it? Nothing to lose. So, I splashed around in the pool several nights a week, copying other learners like me, trying to improve. The mixed-sex sessions seemed odd, so I avoided embarrassment by ignoring the other swimmers and keeping my head down. I concentrated on learning and avoiding bumping into other bodies doing the same. Some swimmers stood in groups talking, which annoyed me as I swam around the obstacle. *What's the point of them coming here?* Eventually, I managed a width, then a length, and was pleased with my progress.

One evening, I got carried away doing the extra little bit and was late leaving the pool. The proficient swimmers were walking in. As I walked past them, one of them said, "Hi, Ali." I didn't recognise the young lady until she said, "Margaret."

Her hair was covered with a tight-fitting black swimming cap, and she wore no make-up. She appeared much shorter and younger than the Margaret I met in the pub. Not knowing where to look, I gazed at her bare feet. *Of course, she was wearing high heels before.* She wore a black swimming costume with vertical white lines following the contours of her body, emphasising her female shape. She didn't seem at all embarrassed, unlike me. I didn't know where to look or place my hands, I felt naked. I said, "Hello, do you come here often?" *What a crass thing to say!*

"I've heard that line before," she replied, smiling. "Yes, almost every session."

"We might bump into each other again, then?"

"It's possible," she said as she walked away.

I changed quickly and decided to watch the proficient swimmers perform. I could learn from them was my excuse to myself. I sat on the back row of benches in the viewing gallery, high above the pool, so I could not be seen. I felt a little creepy, a voyeur, maybe? I was only interested in one swimmer; the pool was now divided into lanes, and there appeared to be etiquette. The disciplined swimmers moved out of each other's way, keeping to one side of the designated separated lanes, unlike the mayhem at the learners' session. They were swimming, tumbling turns at each end of the pool, not splashing and gasping for breath like me. *Which one is Margaret?* The females looked the same from my vantage point, mostly in black costumes. Then, one of the females reached the side and pulled herself out of the water in one movement to a standing position. It was Margaret. I watched as she stretched her arms to the ceiling and touched her toes. Then, she stood at the very edge of the pool with her toes curled around it for grip. Then, she arched her body forward, fingers touching toes, and sprung off the poolside into the water, hardly making a splash. I saw through the water as she pulled her arms down to her sides and back into the diving position. She glided with no effort until she emerged at the surface. Compared to my struggle, her strokes appeared lazy. Reaching the other side of the pool in seconds, a tumble turn, swimming back to the other side effortlessly. After each tumble turn, her stroke changed. She had the entire stroke repertoire, gliding through the water like a fish. Watching Margaret swim made me realise I had to up my game. I wasn't swimming but floundering.

The pool attendant often watched me. Once leaving the pool, he said, "Concentrate on your breathing. The water is not an opponent; use it, don't fight it."

I tried taking his advice, slowed down my stroke, and breathed on every other one, which seemed to help. For some unknown reason, I felt someone was watching me. I looked towards the viewing gallery and saw Margaret standing at the front. I felt embarrassed as she observed my poor technique. Then she waved to me, and I sheepishly waved back to her. Then she pointed to her watch, held both hands up, indicating ten minutes, and made a charade of drinking from a cup, then gave me the thumbs-up. *Why? Why not?* I gave a thumbs-up back.

I was extremely nervous when we met in the little café beside the swimming pool. Margaret smiled, stood up and held her hand for me to shake, so I tentatively touched her fingers. She wore blue jeans, a white T-shirt and trainers, her hair pulled back in a ponytail. I towered over her by a foot in height. *All that elegant power from such a small frame.*

She warmly said, "Hello."

I replied awkwardly, "Hi."

She pointed to a chair. Two cups of coffee were on the table. "Americano, okay?"

I replied, "Fine." I sat down nervously. *Why does this beautiful, confident lady want to talk to me?*

"I hope you don't think I am forward in approaching you. I thought that we could be of help to each other a little."

"In what way?"

Margaret took a deep breath and looked directly into my eyes. "I hope you don't mind me saying you are an Arab, correct?"

The lights in the cafe were very bright, which made her eyes appear larger and even bluer. So much so that I lost concentration. *Why so blue?* I realised I hadn't answered her question immediately and said, "Sorry. Yes, and proud of it."

"That's good. Are you a Muslim?"

Puzzled, I replied, "Of course I am."

"What sect?"

"Sunni... Why are you asking these questions?"

"Sorry if it sounds like an interrogation. Am I offending you? Shall I stop?"

"Sorry if I sounded sharp, but I am curious about the questions; just tell me what you want."

"Okay, here goes; I am studying Middle East history. You are from the Middle East, fluent in Arabic, yes?"

"Arabic, yes, history, not so much."

"You will be surprised at how much you know without realising it, so you could help me."

"You did start by saying we could help each other. How can you help me?"

"I hope this will not offend you, but your spoken English is fair, so your written English should be poor, correct?"

"Yes, it's not very good; George helps me a little."

"I will help you with your English; you help me with your Arabic. How does that sound? So, do we have a deal?"

"Yes, it sounds good, but a little unfair to you as I know so little."

"Can we shake hands on it, then?"

"Sure, why not? Would you like another coffee?"

"That would be lovely."

Her eyes locked on mine as I held her fingers. I was hooked.

We met regularly, sometimes in a coffee shop or, if it was busy, on the banks of the River Isis. We avoided the student rooms at the uni as it was our little secret. Hooked, then captivated by her, the time we spent together was never long enough. So close to her but so far away, if she had been a male I was fond of, a hug, maybe a kiss on both cheeks, would have been appropriate. I was increasingly unable to control myself when I was around her. I hope she didn't notice.

At one of my infrequent meals with George, I plucked up the courage to ask about women, as he didn't seem to have an issue. "I'm meeting a woman who stirred up feelings I found hard to control."

He advised, "Like all animals, our instincts are to mate. Though we differ in a way from most animals, they secrete pheromones from glands to attract a partner. Following their noses, they know exactly where they are when finding a mate. Mating is far more subtle for humans as we no longer mate just for breeding but for pleasure. Signals from interested human mates are received in our brains without our knowledge. Sometimes our brains get it completely wrong, thus causing embarrassing moments."

"So, how do you tell if someone is interested in you?"

"It all depends. Some make it evident by looks, words, or body language; they're my type, as I don't like to be messed about."

"If I am not getting any of those messages, does that mean she isn't interested?"

"Not necessarily. She could be shy, like you, and waiting for you to make the first move. Some women are like that. I avoid them myself. Too much effort."

"I am Muslim. What I feel goes against all my teachings."

"I can't help you there. It's your life. You only come this way once. Your decision. Anyway, who is the lady in question?"

"You remember the night we went to the quiz? It's her, Margaret, one of the women who sat at our table."

"You mean the ice maiden? I wouldn't touch her with a barge pole."

Annoyed by what he said, I angrily asked, "Why?"

"I get no vibes from her. Not my type."

"From what I've seen of your type, that's a good thing, right?"

"Ali, we will not fall out over a woman, okay?" After a short pause, I saw he was as annoyed as I was. George said, "You've got to take the bull by the horns or, to put it another way, a faint heart never won a fair maiden, especially an ice one."

"How do I do that?"

"Make a move, accidentally touch her, see if she is startled and moves away, and go from there. She might get bored if you don't make a move soon."

I rang my father at least once a week; he constantly questioned me about the mosque. Had I made many good Muslim friends? I always replied, 'Baba, I am studying so hard I haven't time for a social life."

"But you are attending the mosque three times a day? That comes first before studying, yes?"

"Baba, it's impossible to attend as often as I like; it's different here. Adhan (call to prayer) is either during a lecture or in the middle of the night, so I go whenever possible, around lunchtime or early evening. But I pray to myself whenever I hear adhan."

"Do you use your prayer mat?"

"Of course, Baba."

That was the first time I lied directly to him. I didn't always use my prayer mat, and I didn't always pray, but I did pray to Allah whenever I heard the call to prayer, which wasn't often. I made up for it at night in my room and prayed alone, but not always.

After attending adhan as a young man in Aleppo with fellow obedient Muslims, I missed the feeling of well-being. The elation slowly disappeared during the day but was repeated at every call to prayer. My conscience wrestled with why I was now drawn more to Margaret than Allah. Unlike adhan, the attraction to Margaret was there all the time. Not just when I was summoned. Walking out of the mosque, I felt content that I had fulfilled my duty. Walking away from Margaret, I felt downhearted, not elated; the urge to stay was compelling. The evident elation I felt when we met seemed to be reciprocated; Margaret's face lit up too. *She feels as I do.*

I reflected on George's advice, weighing his options against my feelings, some of which were too embarrassing to tell him. I made the first move, disregarding all my teachings and Baba's warnings. I didn't feel it was sinful; my conscience was clear that I was doing nothing wrong.

The next time I was out with Margaret I seized my chance and took a risk. Entering a coffee shop, I opened the door and touched her back to guide her through. She turned, looked into my eyes, smiled, and said, "Thank you."

Later that day, we were strolling along the banks of the Isis side by side. Margaret asked questions about life in Syria, as usual. Our hands accidentally brushed; she curled her little finger around mine. Slowly, finger by finger, we held hands like the other couples walking along the towpath. We both turned our heads and looked at each other. She smiled and said, "That's nice."

Something occurred; uncontrolled elation stirred inside me. Margaret then turned to face me, still holding my hand. We were so close I wanted to embrace her. George had said our brains pick up messages without us realising. Something had passed between us. *George was correct.* I could feel it.

She looked at me and said, "I know what you are going through."

"Regarding what?" *Try not to make your emotions obvious.*

She gave me a knowing look. Over time, I discovered she thought she could read my mind. "Your upbringing, faith, is saying what you feel is wrong."

"How do you know that?"

"Because I feel precisely the same."

"You are not Muslim, are you?"

"No, I am not; I have no faith, but I had a strict childhood and was taught right from wrong."

"So, you know what I feel for you is wrong?"

"Yes and no, my upbringing says yes, heart says no."

"I feel the same. I feel different when you are close. My teaching says that it's wrong, too. Could it be the devil tempting us?"

"Ali, there is no such thing as a devil. We must decide whether we continue seeing each other."

"What, now, this minute?"

"Yes, right now."

"Why now?"

"Because it will get more challenging for us not to show each other what we feel.

"How? Who decides?"

"We both do. Walk away from me and sit on the bank of the river and think. I will do the same. When you have decided, come back to me and say either yes or no."

"I don't need to walk away."

"Yes, you do. Please think it through."

I did as she requested and sat on the riverbank for a while; there is something about watching rippling water that facilitates concentration. I had made up my mind before I sat down. The rippling water hadn't changed anything.

Margaret didn't hear me approach, so she was slightly startled when I tapped her shoulder. She stood and faced me. I said, "Yes." She threw her arms around my shoulders and hugged me tightly. This was my first time embracing a woman, so I hugged her gently.

I was surprised that she embraced me strongly, joyfully repeating, "Is your answer yes?"

Bewildered by her response, I repeated, "Yes."

"You can kiss me now to seal it." So, I gently kissed her on both cheeks. "Not like that." She pulled my face onto hers, and we kissed.

I squeezed her as hard as she did me. The warnings or doubts seeded in my head that this wrong vanished and were replaced by euphoria. I didn't want to let go and felt she didn't either.

Arms around each other, we walked back to her flat, knowing something had changed.

"You can come for a coffee if you like."

I was instructed men and women, unless related, were not allowed to be alone and were considered sinful. My inhibitions were still there, so I was nervous about the offer.

Margaret could see my apprehension. Smiling, she looked into my eyes and understood. "It's up to you; coffee, that's all."

Her flat was different from mine in so many ways. She told me it was called a studio flat. It was on the first floor, bigger than mine and had a small kitchen, separated from the main room, with a breakfast bar and a couple of stools. In the bay window was a small writing desk with a swivel chair. Opposite was a comfortable wing-backed chair, placed so the television mounted on the wall could be watched. The room was dominated by a double bed, with cushions strewn across it to make it appear inviting. The matching colours of the curtains, cushions, and table lamps gave the room a warm, inviting glow. Whereas my apartment was bare and functional, Margaret's had feminine touches that matched her warm personality – bright and colourful.

There was another door close to the flat entrance door. Margaret pointed to it, saying at the same time, "If you need to go. Make yourself at home; sit in the bay if you like. I will make you a coffee. Americano okay?"

"Anything," I replied nervously.

Noticing I was still nervous, she countered, "You are the first man to enter my room. I think you should know that."

Margaret sat cross-legged on the bed, propped up with numerous cushions, sipping her coffee. I was taking in the room's ambience, avoiding eye contact with her. "I had better go; it's getting late."

"But it's just starting to rain heavily. Stay a bit longer if you like."

"Raining?" I pulled the curtains back to check, puzzled. I replied, "No, it's not."

This was the first time I saw Margaret's mischievous grin as she said in return, "It's as good an excuse as any."

I could feel her eyes studying me, waiting for my reaction. *Why is my heart pounding? The exhilaration is uncontrollable; what do I do?* I pretended to look out the window again and said, "Floods of a biblical proportion." *Why did I say that?* She tapped the bed beside her. Gingerly, I sat beside her. "I have no experience in this sort of thing."

"Neither have I." Frowning nervously, she added, "My first time too."

"Really, I thought…"

"Yes, really, you thought what?"

"Nothing."

We sat, then laid together that night, two people as one. I had often imagined what it was like to make love. But what happened that night to me was not akin to my imagination. Earlier expectations were about the gratification I would receive. Instead, the joy I received from Margaret's sensuality heightened my own. It was as though our bodies were locked together in wonder and ecstasy. We fell asleep briefly, only to be aroused by our mutual desire for more pleasure.

In the morning, Margaret's face was close to mine. She was playfully plucking my lips with a finger, making an annoying pop-pop noise to rouse me from sleep. "That wasn't half bad, was it?"

Only half bad? What was she expecting? I never expected anything to be so wonderful. "Sorry, it wasn't up to your expectations."

"Ali, it far exceeded anything I had ever dreamt of."

"But you said half bad?"

"Don't be silly; it's a quirky English saying, which means I never expected it to be that good."

"Oh, it would have been easier just to say that."

"Sorry, Ali, it was absolutely wonderful, wasn't it?"

"It was okay," I said jokingly.

"Okay? That's all? Practice makes perfect, you know. We will have to work on that then."

We did practise a lot over the coming days, though nothing could have bettered my first time. We didn't leave her flat for days, eating, sleeping, practising, and talking.

On one of our talking interludes, I asked Margaret, "You remember George inviting us in for a nightcap? Is that one of your weird English expressions?"

"Yes, there are loads of them, some dating back hundreds of years."

"I can't work out why it's called a nightcap? Is that something worn on the head at night?"

"Yes, it used to be the fashion. When it was cold years ago, people used to wear them in bed to keep their heads warm to induce sleep. Later, people discovered a warm drink laced with alcohol could do a better job; hence, nightcap became a drink."

"So, George was inviting us in for a drink?"

"No, not really. He hoped only one of us would accept."

"Why would he only want one of us?"

"Ali, you are so naïve. 'Nightcap' is an innuendo. George meant something entirely different."

"Innuendo, what's that?"

"It's a suggestive remark, sort of code that means something entirely different. The tomcat was asking if Kirstie would like a shag."

"Shag? Why shag? That's a bird, isn't it? Or is that another innuendo?"

"Yes, afraid so, you're right on both counts."

"Why can't you English just say what you mean."

"Because making love is too nice, and a fuck is too coarse, so somebody invented a word for casual sex and thought 'shag' fitted the bill."

"Is 'fitted the bill' another innuendo? No need to answer that, but why shag? A sea bird of all things."

"I have no idea, but be careful. You can quite easily misconstrue a conversation by dropping in an innuendo unintentionally. For instance, 'I watched a couple of shags in broad daylight' or something similar."

"So, George took Kirstie back to his flat for sex? And he had only just met her!"

"Bravo, we finally got there."

"It's a good job I didn't accept the offer and spoil their fun."

"Ali, you were never invited, though some people do like that sort of thing."

"Like an orgy, you mean?"

"Exactly."

"Margaret?"

"Yes?"

"Why does George call the girls he takes back to his room birds? Is that another innuendo for shag?"

"No, and I don't know why young men call girls birds; maybe it's because they're flighty."

"The English language is bonkers."

"Yes, it certainly is, and my last remark was supposed to be funny. They do have jokes in Arabic. Please tell me they do."

"We have funny stories handed down over generations."

Fascinated by Margaret, I wanted to know everything about her. She wanted to know all about me. During our time together, I learned more about her than I did about anyone I had ever known. When we lay together after making love, Margaret reluctantly agreed to tell me her life story on the condition that I told her mine. We lay side by side on the bed. Margaret stared at the ceiling. I lay beside her, lying on my side, head propped up by my hand, my other hand stroking her arm to comfort her. I watched her face as her expression changed. She was uncomfortable telling me about some parts of her life. As she spoke, I watched her face; her expression changed from thoughtful to sad, eyes opening and closing, concentrating on the same spot on the ceiling. She was not the confident, calm woman I thought she was, but vulnerable as her voice trembled nervously as she bared her soul to me.

"We lived in a small cottage on the Kent Marshes. My childhood was full of love, though my mum was strict. If her rules were obeyed, everything was idyllic. I didn't realise something was not right until I was teased at school. A classmate had learned I had no father; kids can be cruel, so I was often bullied."

"Why would they bully you? It wasn't your fault."

"If kids find a weakness, they exploit it, especially girls."

"Not how I was raised. We support each other; it's part of our religion."

"I asked Mother why I didn't have a daddy like other children. Her answer was he wanted to be with us but couldn't because he worked for the government abroad on important business. I believed her. My mum never worked. She looked after the cottage and pretty garden. We never needed anything. When I was about 14 years of age, my mummy became ill. Our doctor asked me to stay away from school for a little while to look after her. Then she was taken to hospital where she soon died. At the funeral, there were just a few neighbours and me. After the funeral, Mum's solicitor, Mr Morris, took me to one side and told me I would attend a convent school and continue my education there. My father occupied my mind most of the time. Where was he? Didn't he care? I dreamt that he would come and take me away. My time at the convent school was horrible."

"Why horrible? It was a religious school, wasn't it."

"It was run by nuns; they were not very understanding. Their rules had to be followed. They had a rule for everything. I think they invented most of them."

"They were teaching you discipline, weren't they?"

"Whatever it was, it wasn't pleasant. I was utterly alone, with nobody to confide in. My past experiences taught me to keep my feelings to myself.

"I started swimming as therapy; I swam and swam, and it focused my mind and used most of my free time. I was in my own little world. The other girls went home during the term holidays, and I stayed there alone. A couple of nuns were friendly, but we had nothing in common. I wondered why my father could be so callous and not take me away from this terrible place.

"As I got older, some strange phrases my mum had used would come to mind. I looked them up and discovered they were Arabic. Mum's hair was fair, not jet-black like mine. She had the same blue eyes as me, so I deduced that perhaps my father was Arabic. That would explain my complexion, too; it's like yours, where it's not covered in black hair like yours.

"When it came to leaving the convent, Mr Morris gave me a letter containing the deeds for the cottage and a bank card that I could use for expenses. A gardener-cum-handyman employed by Mr Morris always looked after the place and still does. The solicitor explained that the bank account would show a balance of £10,000 if used sensibly. The upkeep of the cottage, bills and everything comes from my allowance. I asked him where the money was coming from. He told me it was from my estate and a private matter. I wondered if the money had been left in my mother's will, perhaps from her stepparents or my father. I pleaded with him, but he said it was private. I asked him if it was my father and why I couldn't see him. All sorts of ideas crossed my mind about why he wouldn't see me; maybe he was no longer alive, or was I a secret love child? So, when I enrolled at uni, I chose to study Arabic language and culture to try and get closer to who I believed my father could be."

Margaret turned and faced me. Her expression changed into a mischievous one. Grinning, wiping tears away, she blurted, "That's why I ambushed you. I need a father figure and an Arab. I thought you would do at a push. Come on, Ali, it's your turn; tell me about your mysterious life. For instance, how many camels would I be worth?"

"There's not much to tell, quite boring, but as far as your worth, because of your unruly nature, we are talking about goats, not camels."

"Ha ha, see, you can tell jokes," she said sarcastically but smiling.

We changed positions. I lay on my back, looking at the ceiling, trying to find something interesting to say. Margaret adopted the same position as I had. I stared at the same flaw on the ceiling. Her eyes were glued to my face, and her finger traced my torso. It tickled, and, at times, I trembled when she deliberately tried to distract me.

"Well, here goes my boring life. I live outside Aleppo with my mother, father, older brother, and younger sister… If you want to hear my story, keep your hands to yourself. I can only concentrate on one thing at a time."

"Sorry." She grinned. "I didn't realise it affected you that much. Can't you multitask like me, then?"

"My father buys and sells traditional handmade carpets, and my older brother helps. We are quite well-off compared to some. My mother and sister look after the home, and soon, my sister will be married. I did okay at school; my father could afford further education, which suited me. I was good at sports, in particular freestyle wrestling. At one of the college tournaments, I was spotted by an army recruitment officer looking for suitable recruits. I was encouraged to join the army with the offer of further education. After my initial training, I was singled out for additional education. So that is the reason I am here in Oxford. So there you have it."

"There must be more than that," she teased as her fingers explored more sensitive areas. "Wrestling? You can't even tame a feeble little girl."

I moved onto my side, saying simultaneously, "This is my favourite hold; try and get out of this." I slipped my arm around her waist.

"That's easy," she said matter-of-factly as her hand moved.

I submitted, saying, "Nobody has ever tried that move before."

Later, she asked, "They call moves by different names, don't they?"

"Yes, they do. It's not like the rehearsed stuff you watch on the television; freestyle is entirely different."

"So, what would you call that submission move I just did?"

"An illegal move."

I was back at my flat collecting clothes and stuff when my phone rang. It was Margaret; I was surprised as it was only a brief time since I left hers. "Margaret, missing me already?"

I was expecting something similar in reply, but what she said startled and confused me, first by the sharp tone of her voice and then by what she said. "We can't see each other anymore; please don't try and contact me. Sorry, goodbye." I could tell by her voice she was distraught.

So, I rang back at once, but there was no answer. *What have I done wrong?* I kept trying all afternoon until the line became permanently engaged.

I tapped on George's door, hoping he was alone. He was for a change. He looked tired; he would never admit it was from studying. He could see I was upset, so he offered me into his dimly lit room. The only light on was over his table, covered in open books and notepads. *So, he does work sometimes.*

"You look like shit," was his opening remark. "What's up?"

"I don't know, everything was wonderful this morning then, for no reason, she doesn't want to see me again."

"Are we talking about the 'ice maiden'?"

"Margaret, yeah, but she isn't an 'ice maiden'."

"Spill the beans. Has she bombed you out? She has, hasn't she?"

"She told me it's all over for no reason. I can't work it out."

"Well, I did warn you, didn't I? She is playing a game with you. Testing you out. She is after commitment, wants you to make promises, and has got you by the balls.

Take my advice, don't play along with it. It will end in tears regardless."

"She is not like the girls you sleep with. She's not like them. She's different."

"I don't know what you mean by different; all the girls I bed are the same. They know what I want, and they know what they want."

"What should I do, or what can I do?"

"Thank your lucky stars, and move on; there's plenty of fish in the sea."

"What if I don't want to move on?"

"You will learn the hard way; in the end, that's what will happen."

I went back to my room and racked my brains. *What could I possibly have done?*

I hardly slept that night, deliberating on what I could have done wrong. The words Margaret spoke and George's advice reverberated in my head. In the morning, I concluded she would tell me what I had done, no matter what. So, I telephoned her flat, time and time again, but it just rang and rang. *Something is seriously wrong.* Then I had a brainwave. *George might have Kirstie's phone number.*

He reluctantly gave it to me. Kirstie was very understanding and offered to meet me outside Margaret's flat. I stood back when Kirstie rang the bell to not be seen if she looked out the window.

Margaret opened the door. I jammed it open with my foot. Margaret said appealingly, "Please go. It's over; there's no point." She glared at Kirstie and said, "What the fuck are you doing here?"

"Sorry, Kirstie, do you mind going? I just need to talk to her."

"Ali, she's all screwed up. I would leave it for now." She curled her finger at me, repeating 'now', moving her head sideways, indicating that was my best option.

I pushed open the entrance door and got to Margaret's flat door before she could slam it in my face. I forced past her and closed the door behind us so she was trapped in the room with me. "All I want is an explanation, please. I am owed that, don't you think?"

"Just go; we can't go on like this."

"Like this? You were fine a couple of hours ago. Are you playing a game with me? Testing me? What are you up to?"

Margaret's expression changed. She looked angry and raised her voice for the first time. "How many times do you have to be told it's over."

"Only once, with a good reason. I need to know what I have done!"

"You haven't done anything; it's me."

"Okay, what have you done? Tell me, what's so bad."

"I lied to you; that's what I have done. A relationship can't be built on lies."

"Let me be the judge of that. Please, it's the least you can do; tell me."

"If I tell you, you will leave, yes?"

"If that's what you want."

Margaret took a deep breath. "Okay, but before I start, I want to apologise for misleading you." My throat was dry, so I poured two glasses of water and passed one to Margaret. "I told you that my mother died, but I didn't tell you the circumstances, did I."

"No, I can't see what this has to do with our relationship."

Margaret sat cross-legged on the bed. I sat in the window chair. "Mother died of ovarian cancer. When I left the convent and returned to my cottage, I reregistered with my local doctor. He suggested testing me to see if the cancer was familial. He said when Mum died that 'Lynch syndrome' was suspected."

Oh shit, she will tell me she's dying of cancer? "Lynch syndrome? What's that?"

"It's a genetic condition where a parent passes the disease on to their children."

Oh no, she has cancer. "So, you're going to tell me you have cancer, yes?"

"No, listen, please, stop interrupting."

"My doctor advised me the tests showed that the markers were there for the same aggressive cancer that killed my mother."

"Shit."

"The hospital consultant left the decision up to me. He told me the prognosis of ignoring the diagnoses or intervention was a normal life or possible premature death. The decision was ultimately mine. At the time, the solution was easy: I wanted to live. So, I had an operation to remove my ovaries and fallopian tubes. So, I avoided relationships as they couldn't lead anywhere anyway. Like your mate, George, says, I became an 'ice maiden'. My character changed. I erected a barrier to stop anyone from getting in. Until you came along and jumped the barrier and captivated me. I wasn't strong enough to resist you. As soon as you walked out of the door, I felt shame and guilt at not being completely honest. So, there you have it."

"Wow!"

Margaret sobbed. "Yes, Wow!"

"My flatmate, George, gave me some advice; he simply told me to 'live for today'. I think it's good advice. I didn't take it on board till now."

"George, you're taking advice from George. Who has the morals of a tom cat."

"Margaret, please listen. I was raised to believe what we are doing is sinful. In my country, we could be stoned to death. If we 'live for today', we will deal with tomorrow when it comes, hopefully never. Who knows what tomorrow brings?"

"Ali, I have never felt like this about anyone before, so not telling you everything was disrespectful. You deserved the truth because I love you. As the saying goes, 'like mother, like daughter'."

I sat beside Margaret on the bed, my arms around her shoulders. She felt rigid and didn't move towards me, so I gently pulled her head onto my shoulder. She became less stiff, and her sobs got louder, then stopped.

"It's time to go now; you know everything."

"You haven't been listening; I am not going anywhere. You are not getting rid of me that easily."

"But there is no future. I can never be a complete woman."

"The future can wait. I want you now. We can make our own future."

"Ali, we have only known each other properly for a few days. Be serious."

"Let me stay tonight; we can talk it through. You can try and convince me why not, and I will try to convince you why."

"The longer you are in my room, the harder it will be for me, so please go now." Margaret got off the bed and gestured for me to leave.

"I don't want to go. I have choices too, don't I?"

"If you still want to be with me, promise that if at any time it's over, tell me, don't just walk away."

"That will never happen; come here so I can hold you."

Margaret's tears prompted mine, and we both looked at each other, waiting for the other to move. Margaret didn't respond, so I did. I held her gently, laid her on the bed, and pulled her head onto my chest. I felt so tired and weary. We fell asleep together; she must have felt the same.

We slept together that night like a pair of spoons. I was awoken when Margaret turned to face me. Her fingers traced down my forehead along my nose and touched my lips. This would become the way if she woke up first to awaken me. I looked into her eyes, uncertain of what she was thinking.

Then Margaret spoke. Her eyes never left mine; she looked earnest and sincere. "George was right; live for today. Can we try?"

Imitating the echoing sincerity in Margaret's voice and eyes, I replied, "It's the only way. Tomorrow never comes."

Things changed slowly between us in the following weeks as we began to understand each other. Margaret's confidence returned, and her funny, mischievous traits reappeared. We had made our pact; either of us could break it anytime. We became an unlikely couple of misfits. I had total trust in her and felt it was reciprocated.

Chapter 3

Detective Work

We visited Margaret's little cottage in the Kent Marshes whenever we could. One evening, we sat on the hearth rug in front of the open log fire, watching the red cracking sparks disappear up the chimney, the lights turned down low, drinking a glass or two of red wine. Leaning against a sofa facing the fire, Margaret lay sideways to me, her head on my lap. *What could be better than this? What would my family make of it?*

Thankfully, these cringing thoughts were brought to an abrupt end as Margaret interrupted, "You are the first man I have really got to know; I thought you should know that."

"Touché. First woman, of course."

"Sitting here like this makes me think of my father. I hope he is like you."

"Thanks for the compliment."

"Am I ever going to solve the issue of who he is?"

I didn't reply. *Sometimes, it's for the better, but it's best to know, or is it?* A lightbulb idea came to mind. "I think you need to solve who your mother is first."

"Don't be silly. I know who my mum is."

"Really, who is she?

"My mum is my mum."

"So, if you know all about her, what was she doing before you were born? More importantly, where was she when she got pregnant?"

"She never told me anything like that. I was only a child."

"Exactly, so we need to find out who your mum was. Possibly, that could lead to your father."

"Okay, Detective Mansour, where do we start?"

"Right here, in this cottage where she lived, there must be paperwork somewhere."

"If there is, I haven't seen any."

"Have you looked?"

"Of course I have looked, not really searched though, but I would have come across things unless they're hidden."

"There must be some paperwork somewhere, surely?"

"Come on then, let's do some exploring."

"What, now? Can't it wait till tomorrow, Margaret, please?"

"No, now, it's a challenge. I won't sleep otherwise. I think the best place would be to start in Mum's bedroom."

We searched the house from top to bottom and found nothing of interest. It was a stone cottage, so I tapped my knuckles on the walls, hoping to find secret cupboards. We checked the backs of cabinets and wardrobes for concealed storage and found nothing.

"There is no paperwork anywhere. I find that strange; there must be some, somewhere."

"Perhaps my mum's solicitor would have something about her, but he wasn't accommodating the last time I asked."

"Okay, I will look in the loft tomorrow morning, the only place we haven't searched. You never know what we'll find."

"Why can't we look now?"

"Because it's late, I have had a couple of glasses of wine, and the loft will still be there in the morning."

"Straight after breakfast, promise?"

"Yes, okay, but don't set the alarm clock."

"No need. I'll be awake early; I wonder what's up there?"

"Other than bats and cobwebs, you mean?"

The loft hatch door surprisingly had a pull-down ladder attached, which Margaret told me she had never seen before. *Interesting.* The loft space was tidier and cleaner than I expected. A large metal-bound wooden chest was placed close to the hatch, within easy reach of the ladder. It was heavy. *Too heavy for a woman to carry?* I slid the chest through the hatch, used the ladder as a slide to carefully lower it and placed it on the floor.

Margaret's face was a picture of excitement. Impatiently, she opened the lid, exclaiming, "It's full of paper, books and things!"

"Margaret, please wait; let's do this slowly and methodically."

"But it's so exciting. I can't wait to see what's inside. I feel like a child at Christmas!"

"I wouldn't know about that; let me. Better still, help me get the chest downstairs." We slid the chest down the stairs, one step at a time, me in front taking the weight.

We set up a workstation downstairs on the dining table; Margaret had a notepad so everything could be recorded neatly and placed in order of importance. The idea was to make an itinerary of what we found between us before moving to the next item.

That was the plan, but things of no interest were put aside quickly without noting as Margaret's eagerness took hold. There was so much stuff that we decided to change tack and only look for items that preceded Margaret's birth by a year. It was time-consuming, but we slowly built up a picture of Margaret's mother, Carol Fraser. She was an orphan. Fraser was the family's name that adopted and raised her as their child. Death certificates and funeral orders of service proved that her foster parents were deceased, but there was no information on her real parents. We decided that now wasn't the time to pursue this. Carol's school reports were put to one side to peruse later. They did show she went to a grammar school for girls and did well. She started work in the City of London as an assistant to a director of a large oil company. So, we trawled through all the oil company's papers until a year before Margaret was born. We came across a bundle of papers tied with a ribbon. On top of the bundle was a memo regarding a visit from the Syrian ministry of energy, Mr Emre Hamoud. The message confirmed that Carol Fraser was part of the ensemble to guide the minister on a trip to the Pembrokeshire refineries. The memo date was approximately nine and a half months before Margaret's birth. Also, we found a thank you card, with a message that read 'I will never forget you', signed 'E.H.'. Inside the card was a pressed yellow flower Margaret recognised came from a gorse bush.

Margaret exclaimed excitedly, "Jackpot! It's got to be him, hasn't it?"

"Don't get carried away. We need to do some checking before we jump to any conclusions," I said to bring her down to Earth, which failed.

Margaret was now trying to learn as much about Emre Hamoud as possible. Her enthusiasm rubbed off on me, and I was drawn to the challenge.

When we returned to uni, the library archives were our first call. It wasn't challenging to find Emre Hamoud; he was alive and still the minister for energy, though there was little personal stuff on the microfiche database. We spent hours trawling through the microfiche files of old newspapers, concentrating on anything to do with the oil industry without success. Perhaps the visit wasn't as crucial as we initially assumed.

We decided to search through the local Pembrokeshire newspapers as a last resort. We hit the jackpot. Not only was there an article on the trip but a picture too. Though grainy, the names of those in the photo were listed in a short article below. Standing smiling next to Carol Fraser was Emre Hamoud. Margaret needed a better look and magnified Emre Hamoud's face as large as possible. It looked like a mass of dots, unrecognisable as a face.

Margaret, though, could see more than that, exclaiming, "Proof beyond doubt, look at his mass of jet-black hair, unruly just like mine, that's my daddy."

Unsure of what she could see, I tried to subdue her, saying, "Margaret, look at my hair, black and curly. Am I your daddy, too?"

"It's him. I don't care what you say."

I jokingly said, "He's still alive and doing the same job; fancy a visit to Syria."

"Could we? Is it possible?"

"Margaret, I was only joking; it's completely out of the question."

"But there is another way. Perhaps we could have a meeting with your solicitor."

"He wasn't helpful the last time I saw him. He was quite old then. He might not even be alive."

"Worth a try, but don't let on what you want to see him about. Spring it on him."

I accompanied Margaret to Mr Morris's dark, dreary office; he was old, barely alive. I shook his cold, fragile hand, frightened it may break. He was exactly as I had pictured him; small and thin, with grey hair — what was left of it. Gold wire-framed glasses perched on the end of his nose. He started the conversation by politely asking what he could do for us. Margaret requested to see the files he held on her estate. He contacted his receptionist and asked for Margaret Fraser's file to be brought from the archives. Duly delivered, he opened the box file, partitioned into distinct categories. One partition was labelled Carol Fraser, and another had Margaret's name.

Pointing to copies of the cottage deeds and various other documents, Mr Morris imparted, "Unfortunately, that is all I can show you."

Margaret enquired, "Please, Mr Morris, can I see all the documents?"

"As I said, unfortunately, you can't; the information therein is sensitive and not within my realm to disclose."

Margaret pleaded again, "We both know why I want to see the documents. I am not a child anymore. Everyone is entitled to know who their father is, surely, please."

Mr Morris, looking out of the window, didn't answer for a while. He seemed to me to be deep in thought. As though his attention was drawn to what was happening outside. I looked, but there was nothing to see except a lamp post. *Strange.* Then, as though he had just had a lapse of memory, he said, "Sorry, but I have something to deal with. I will be back in five minutes, okay?" As he rose from his chair, he glanced at the files on the table, then at me, uttering, "Back in a mo."

As the door closed, I picked up the box file, removed a confidential clip, and opened the file. We were both scanning the file as quickly as possible. Seeing Hamoud written on the front, we both exclaimed, "Bloody hell!" We flipped through the file's contents, which puzzled both of us as they were copies of the history of Margaret growing up. There were far too many school photos, reports, and medical forms to read, so we quickly skipped through them. Listening and furtively looking for the door opening at the same time. On the very last page, the heading was 'Ali Mansour' and details of me.

Why me? Am I being spied on?

After five minutes, the door partly opened, then closed again, making a squeak. Then the door fully opened a second or two later, and Mr Morris entered the room. Sitting at his desk, he said, "Oh dear, old age doesn't come on its own. I went to the archives and realised I hadn't picked up your file, tut, tut."

Margaret said knowingly, "I am always doing that."

"Is there anything else I could do for you, Miss Fraser?"

"No, thank you, we have all we want. Thanks again for being unhelpful," Margret said, smiling.

Mr Morris replied, "My pleasure."

Margaret couldn't contain herself when we got outside the solicitor's office. She laughed and cried, hugging me, saying, "I have a daddy who cares about me."

I didn't say anything for a while; Margaret was talking too fast, and I wasn't listening. I was concerned she had jumped to the conclusion that Emre Hamoud was her father without a doubt because the name Hamoud was on a file.

Later that evening, when Margaret was less excited, I told her, "All we know is the solicitor was instructed to keep details of you. The name Hamoud was on the front."

"Yes, that's proof enough for me."

"Hamoud is a common surname in Syria like Smith is in the UK. All it proves is that someone with that name could be your father or knows who your father is. Perhaps Hamoud is a solicitor in Syria, collecting information for someone else."

"Ali, it's got to be him. I just know it is."

"Maybe. Sorry to put the kibosh on it, but I think something else is happening. Why were my details in your file?"

"I thought that strange, too. It's as though someone wants to know everything about me. It must be my father. Who else could be interested?"

"Beats me; let's sleep on it."

"I'm too excited for that. Goodnight, Ali, and thank you… It is him."

"We'll see."

Chapter 4

The Syria Trip, 1995

A year had flown by, and the summer holiday was upon us. I had to return to Syria to see my parents and check in at the army training school. Margaret wanted to join me. I realised she might find it difficult in many ways as a woman. She would be in a strange place, and coping with the sweltering temperature and customs would be challenging. I conveyed my concerns to her, but Margaret had the skillfulness to win me over, convincing me she would be fine against all my reservations.

"Look, I am half Arab," she would often say, veiling her face.

"You won't convince anybody with those blue eyes, and that's all they will see."

She got her way. I warned my parents that I was bringing a friend and asked if that was okay. Mentioning my friend was a woman would have been too difficult to explain. I hoped when they met her, they would see what I saw. I told Margaret how to behave, coaching her not to be tactile with me or any male family member and to try to be demure. So, the trip was booked.

Introducing Margaret to my family was going to be difficult. So we decided to get it over with as soon as possible. When I approached my family home, I realised how difficult it would be and knocked on the door in trepidation. Baba opened it and cried excitedly, "It's Ali!"

I was swarmed by hugs and kisses from Baba, Mama, my brother, Abdul, and my sister, Arwa. I had momentarily forgotten about Margaret. When the greetings had almost stopped, I raised my hands and said, "Enough. I would like you to meet my friend, Margaret."

Silence fell; my family looked shocked, and their stony faces glared at me like I was insane. They made no effort to greet Margaret; Baba waved me into the house and gave an over-exaggerated irritated wave to Margaret to enter. Margaret froze. I tried to encourage her to join us, but I saw she was alarmed, so I automatically held out my hand. She held it and smiled with relief. I immediately realised it was a mistake, seeing my family's reaction of anger and bewilderment.

My baba guided me into the male quarter of the house, and my mama and Arwa herded Margaret into the female quarter. Baba stood in front of me, not offering a place to sit. I had never seen him so angry. His loud, penetrating voice yelled, "Why have you brought this unclean woman into our home? Tell me what excuse you could have?"

"She is my friend, and I am offended you called her unclean. Please don't shout; she will hear you."

Still shouting, he replied, "Is she a Muslim? I know the answer to my question: no Muslim woman travels alone with a man whose family is unrelated. Would she?"

"No, probably not, but that does not make her unclean."

"In my eyes, it does; she cannot stay in this house one moment longer; tell her to go."

"Baba, if she goes, I go too."

"Ali, what have you become? Are you unclean as well?"

"Not in my eyes, Baba. I have done nothing wrong, nor has she."

Baba implored, "Ali, we were so excited to see you and explain our plans. Your mama and Awra have worked hard to make your visit special."

"Sorry if I have spoilt your plans, Baba," I replied sarcastically.

"Abni (son), your mama and sister have found a good girl for you to marry. It's arranged. The dowry has been agreed upon. She is an excellent, strong, obedient girl. At 14 years of age, she is perfect for you. She will bear you many children."

"Baba, I will choose my own wife. You should have asked me first."

"Abni, it's always the way; a child cannot know better than their mama in such things."

"You should have asked, Baba. I will not marry someone I don't know."

"You're shaming our family; it goes against our religion and traditions. I knew it was a mistake letting you go to that evil country. You have always been weak."

"Baba, please let me make up my mind about who I marry."

"Get out of my site, take that prostitute with you, and never come back. You are not my son; shame on you and our family. Go now."

I marched out of Baba's lounge into the women's quarters. Without knocking on the door, I pushed it open. Mama and Awra glared at Margaret on the opposite side of the room. Apparently, they had not offered Margaret a place to sit or offered refreshments, which was our custom. Margaret was standing and looking out of the window; she turned to me and nervously, knowingly smiled. I showed her my hand, and she took it without hesitation. My mama and sister hissed like snakes as we left the room holding hands.

Margaret, shaking, uttered quietly, out of earshot of the family, "What the fuck is going on?"

"The prodigal son returning didn't go exactly as planned," I said, trying to underplay what had just happened.

Margaret replied, "I heard everything your father said about me and was upset for you."

"It's my fault. I never should have brought you here."

"If you hadn't, you would have been betrothed to a 14-year-old."

"Yes, and married soon if I hadn't met you."

"I bet you regret that now."

"I have changed because of you, all for the better, not by that evil country, as my father said."

"He will come round; you are his son, after all."

"Afraid not. My family will never change. I am no longer part of them. I have disgraced them. If they had the opportunity, they would queue to throw the first stone."

"Sorry, I have come between you and your family."

"I'm not; you are my family now."

Hugging me, she replied, "You're mine too."

We left Aleppo and returned to Damascus to spend a few days there. I had to check in with the army before returning to Oxford. Which left Margaret time to do some sightseeing, or so I thought. Unknown to me, Margaret had checked out Emre Hamoud and had his office details. She dropped the bombshell that she had already contacted his office requesting an interview with him. The pretext was drafting a thesis on the interaction between Syria's exports and the UK. Margaret explained to the receptionist that she had only a few days left due to unforeseen circumstances. Apologising that her trip had been curtailed, she asked if it would be possible to meet Emre at short notice. Margaret's pleading worked; fortunately – *unfortunately* – she was allowed to interview Emre Hamoud.

Margaret wanted me to take notes at the meeting, insisting it would look more authentic. I worried she didn't understand what she was getting herself into. So, I told her, "We have no idea what type of person Emre Hamoud is; be incredibly careful. Unlike in the UK, there are some things you cannot say; you could be imprisoned if you suggest someone has done something wrong, and they could throw away the key. He is a government minister used to power and control. Even suggesting he fathered a child out of wedlock could be severe punishment. You do understand it is risky in so many ways?"

"Okay, I promise I will not say anything out of place. Promise I'll be careful, will you come? Please?"

"Okay, but if I gesture to stop talking, you will stop and let me take over, yes?"

"Of course I will."

Margaret's reassurance didn't help my doubts because I knew how impulsive and assertive she could be. But I surrendered in the end, as I always did. Though nervous it could all go wrong, I reluctantly followed her plan. A part of me was also curious, but I knew the line we were treading was narrow.

We were shown Emre Hamoud's large modern office; he rose from his executive chair and said, "Good afternoon. What can I do for you?" He indicated we should sit on the chairs on the other side of his immaculately tidy desk. Emre was quite tall and looked like he was reasonably fit for a man his age. His mop of jet-black hair was dusted with silver. His Western clothes and shoes appeared expensive and immaculate. I felt out of place, wearing jeans and a T-shirt. I opted not to wear a thawb, as I wanted to look like an overseas student, which I was.

Margaret was the first to speak. "We are both studying at Oxford University and are jointly drafting a thesis on the integration of the East and the West regarding oil demand and production. Is it okay for my friend, Ali, to take notes?"

Well-rehearsed and going well so far. I watched Emre closely in case Margaret said anything out of place, studying his reaction to Margaret's questions so I could stop them quickly if needed.

After observing us for a few seconds, Emre asked in an open and friendly manner, "How can I help?"

I realised that friendliness can sometimes be used to distract the interviewer; after all, he has been a politician for a long time. I was wary that what appeared to be a welcoming smile had been honed over many years to his advantage. I was close enough to tap Margaret's foot behind the desk if she said anything that could cause an issue. I watched them both as they interacted with each other.

Margaret took a deep breath and replied, "Well, we know from our research that you visited oil refineries in the UK some 20-odd years ago. I wondered how you compared the work ethic between UK and Syrian workers, then and now?"

So good so far.

"Ah, yes, I did visit the UK many years ago. The difference at the time was the UK refineries were more technically advanced. The workers seemed to me to be similarly motivated but more skilled. Since then, we have initiated training programmes and modernised our refineries."

"Was there anything, in particular, you thought to be improved by either country?"

Good question.

"Yes, training in particular. Syria, as I just said, was a long way behind technically." Emre was still looking at Margaret; was he bemused by her? Or unsure where the questions were going?

"What did you think of the refineries in Pembrokeshire regarding their recent modernisation at that time?"

"Ah, first of all, from what I can remember, as it was 20-odd years ago, was what a beautiful area they had chosen. I remember it with affection."

Margaret interjected, "Yes, it is a beautiful area with fantastic beaches."

Where the blazes is she going?

Emre, displeased, said, "Could you please talk about oil, not beaches."

I tapped her foot. "Of course, but did you ever visit Barafundle Bay, one of the most beautiful beaches in the world? Surely you would remember that?

Tap, tap. *What is she up to?*

"Well, as I said, it was about 20 years ago."

Tap, Tap, tap. *Move on.*

Then Margaret dropped her bombshell and, looking at him directly, "20 odd years and nine months, to be exact."

Emre didn't gather what she meant at first; I saw his puzzled face change to annoyed.

"Margaret, we have enough information; please, let's go."

"Okay, Ali, I have just one question. Do you remember one of your guides, a young woman called Carol Fraser?"

Emre slumped in his chair as though hit by a sledgehammer. Confused, he said, "Yes, I remember her well."

Worried she had overstepped the mark, I pleaded, "Margaret, that's enough; we have to leave now."

Emre held out his hand, indicating I should stop talking. "Calm down, young man, please. I am interested in what she says." Emre looked bewildered momentarily as he spoke, "How do you know Carol Fraser?"

Margaret looked directly into Emre's eyes, announcing, "She's my mother."

"Ah, that's it. You have your mother's eyes. I knew there was something about you."

Please, Margaret, don't dig a bigger hole.

Looking at Margaret, he asked, "How is your mother? Well, I hope."

I am confused now and can see Margaret is.

Margaret was taken aback by Emre's question, blurting, "She died when I was 14."

He looked shocked. "Oh, that must have been terrible; being raised by your father as a single parent couldn't have been easy for either of you."

I was right; we have the wrong Hamoud. Panic over?

"I don't have a father."

"Everyone has a father. He must be somewhere."

"Yes, but finding him sometimes is difficult. My mother said he worked abroad."

"How old are you exactly?"

"20 odd years, minus 9 months or so."

Has the penny finally dropped?

Emre looked enlightened, then annoyed and uttered, "So, you think I am your father."

Please don't say yes.

"Yes, I did when I walked into your office, but I don't anymore. I know my real father kept a record of my life, every little detail. He knows my mother died and provided for me, so it's obvious it's not you; sorry if I have caused offence."

Emre looked drained, as though someone had given him the shocking news. *He is concerned about Margaret, not angry at being accused. Strange.*

"Sorry, I can't be of any help with finding your father. That's all you really came for, isn't it?

Be careful how you answer.

"Yes, it was. Thanks for being understanding."

Oh no, the wrong answer.

"I hope you do find him. I can't fully understand why you thought I was your father. Hope you find him."

"I found a card, signed 'E.H.', and a paper clipping of your visit to Pembroke. I put two and two together."

"Sorry, I can't help you further."

Emre must have summoned his secretary; the door opened, and his secretary signalled it was time to leave.

As we left the office, Margaret whispered, "I was sure it was him. Everything fits. If it's not him, who is it?"

"I don't know. You really had me worried in there; I thought he would have at least thrown us out or pressed the alarm bell."

"I thought he was lovely and understanding. I wish he were my father. He is exactly as I dreamed he would be."

"Where did that beach come from? He got a bit bristly when you mentioned it. Did you notice?"

"Yes, I did. I thought his reaction was odd; Barafundle Bay jumped into my head when I spotted a memo on his desk signed 'E.H.'. It looked like the same E.H. on Mum's card to me."

"I still don't get it."

"Well, when I was young, Mum used to take me to Pembrokeshire. We always visited Barafundle Bay and sat high above the beach in the same quiet spot amongst yellow-flowered gorse bushes. Mum used to cut and hold the flower, gazing out to sea. She always looked sad."

"I see, so the initials E.H. on his notepad triggered you to remember E.H. on your mother's card. So, you blurted out Barafundle Bay without thinking... Great?"

"Yes, Ali, that's about it, but his reaction, I thought, was weird."

Walking back to our hotel. I couldn't help looking around, making excuses to stop. Checking that no one was following us.

Margaret was laughing. "What are you doing? Don't be silly. No one is following us."

"I hope not. Emre was hard to read, like a typical politician. Something doesn't add up, though."

"You're a detective now," Margaret said, linking my arm more tightly. Glancing behind, she added, "You've got me doing it now."

The following morning at breakfast, a porter handed an unsigned hotel memo to us: 'Please attend reception asap'.

We looked at each other, and both mouthed *shit*.

Margaret shrugged. "What do we do?"

"There's no option; it isn't a request but an order. I think that we have opened a can of worms."

I apprehensively handed the note to the receptionist, who told us a car was waiting outside. "Where are we going?" I nervously replied.

He said nothing, shrugged his shoulders and pointed to the door.

On the way out of the hotel, I quipped, "On our way to meet your daddy, I hope."

"You think?"

"Your guess is as good as mine."

A black limousine was parked outside, with a chauffeur smoking a cigarette standing alongside. In unison, we both asked, "Where are you taking us?"

"All will become clear soon. No need to worry."

The answer didn't instil any confidence. Margaret looked anxious and was making funny quips as she did when nervous.

The limo parked outside an impressive restaurant. We were guided into a private suite by a porter. Sitting at the dining table was a distinguished-looking lady with slightly greying hair, smartly dressed in a business-style suit. She pointed to two chairs opposite her and gestured for us to sit. She introduced herself as Fatima Hamoud and said, "You must be wondering what this is about, and I will tell you, though it's a long story, so please be patient."

Hamoud?

Margaret blurted, "Is it about my father?"

Doesn't she think before opening her mouth?

"All in good time. I hope you will understand at the end of my story and not think badly of Emre or me, especially me."

Emre? We both looked at each other at the mention of his name.

She rang the service bell and asked for the waiter, who appeared like a genie in seconds. "A pot of coffee for three, please," she asked politely. "Let's begin. Please, if you can, do not butt in until I have finished. All should come clear. My husband is Emre Hamoud; we married many years ago. It was not an arranged marriage; we were both studying at university and became besotted with each other. Both sets of our parents were modern-thinking and reasonably well-off. They discussed our relationship and suggested it would be best we get married before it's too late."

"Too late?" Margaret repeated.

"Please let me continue. I have just begun." Fatima added, "Before we have an unexpected gift."

"Oh, I see, but what has this got to do with us?" Margaret said with a puzzled look.

"Please be patient; as I said, we married, and it was bliss for two years. We were striving for our unexpected gift, but it never came. We tried everything, but nothing seemed to work. So, we decided to see a consultant to discover why we were unlucky. I will not go into the medical details, but I was told that the tests proved I was barren and could never conceive. I went into a bout of depression. I was planning a family of at least three children; Emre encouraged me as he, too, wanted children. I felt like a failure and pushed Emre away. Our loving marriage vanished. Instead of being at home and looking after my children and husband, I became an obsessed career woman. Emre became consumed with work, and our relationship became nothing more than convenient. Due to his efforts, he was appointed the energy minister. I was working for the General Intelligence Directorate and achieved a supervisory role. So, we both did well in our careers, but our personal life was a failure.

"Emre was invited to the UK on political business regarding oil production. When any delegation goes abroad, it is strictly monitored for security reasons. A red flag was raised, naming Carol Fraser as a 'person of interest'. Her relationship with Emre appeared to be over-friendly. We had to run checks on her to discover what her motives were. We could find nothing to suggest an ulterior explanation regarding her friendliness towards Emre other than a mutual attraction to each other. At this point, I took complete control of the surveillance. All reports and correspondence had to come directly to me, so only I knew what was happening between them.

"I became obsessed with their relationship, needing to know every little detail. When Emre returned home, I could see a change in him. He seemed even more distant from me than before. I continued to monitor any correspondence between Emre and Carol. It was apparent they were deeply in love. I became extremely jealous of Carol, as she had what I once had with him. I am not proud of what I did; jealousy was destroying me. I got pleasure from intercepting their letters. Both were pleading with each other to respond. I am ashamed that I did get some satisfaction from this. Then a letter from Carol shattered everything. She was pregnant with Emre's child. Emre's last distraught letter to Carol accused her of using him. He wanted more and was devastated he had been tricked by her. When she got no response from her letter explaining she was carrying his child, begging him to respond, the letters from Carol stopped, as eventually Emre's did.

"I engaged a solicitor to monitor her. So, the events in Carol's life could be forwarded to me discreetly. After you were born, things changed. The child that I wanted with Emre so badly was someone else's. I wanted to tell Emre he had a child but couldn't bring myself to tell him what I had done. I watched you growing up as though you were my child. I did my best to help you and your mother have a comfortable life."

I listened to Fatima's story in disbelief. Her face convinced me her confession was a genuine act of contrition. She drooped her head, eyes closed, waiting for the onslaught from Margaret.

"How could you be so cruel? My mother lived with a broken heart; she hid it from me because of you!" Margaret's face was filled with hate, anger and uncontrollable rage. "It was my mum you punished. You're an evil, selfish woman!"

Fatima sat, head drooped, and feebly said, "I know. I agree. I am so sorry."

"What could possess someone to destroy so many lives because they couldn't bear a child? I can't bear a child, but I would never do what you did."

"I don't know why; I can't explain. I am so sorry. I will tell Emre the truth tonight."

"What happens next?" I said awkwardly, unable to think of the correct words.

Looking at me and ignoring Fatima, Margaret said, "So Emre is my father. I knew it. Ali, I told you, I could feel it."

Fatima raised her head defiantly and said, "Yes, he is. He doesn't know yet for sure. He didn't know about your mother's death until you told him yesterday."

"But he thinks I am his daughter, doesn't he?"

"I think he may have worked it out; if he hasn't, he soon will."

Not so angry, Margaret stared at Fatima. "So you financed Mum and me, sent me to a convent school, and paid for everything. You did all that, and my father knew nothing."

"Yes. I watched you grow up like a mother. I am proud of you and your achievements. It was my guilty pleasure."

"Do you think that made it all right then?"

"No, probably not; I was doing it for me. Guilt is hard to bear on your own."

"So is a broken heart. Didn't you think of what my mother was going through?"

"Yes, I know what it feels like, and I can't say sorry enough, sorry."

"You kept a dossier on me. Why?"

"In case I died, it was to be given to Emre, along with the letters they never received." Fatima placed a box full of letters on the table.

Excitedly, Margaret asked, "Can I read them? Please?"

"Sorry, not yet. That'll be up to your father."

"So, you will tell him the whole truth about who I am?"

"Yes, last night I realised the lie I have been living and how much your mother meant to him. When he came home last night, he went straight to his room. That's not unusual, but he never came out last night."

"Oh my God, what do you think he will say?"

"A range of emotions; he'll be furious with me for ruining so many lives. Mourning for the loss of your mother. Missing you growing up, but unbelievably happy that he now has his child to love."

"How will I know if he wants to see me?"

"He will; I will let you know when."

Margaret's mood changed as she realised Fatima was trying her hardest to put things right. She engaged Fatima face-to-face and said, "It has been difficult for you. I know what it feels like to want a child, to feel incomplete. I can understand what you went through. But I can never forgive you."

"I don't expect you to. It will be different between you and Ali because he knew you could never bear a child. At least you both know from the start and have come to terms with it."

"I feel for Ali. It's not his fault. It's mine. It will slowly dawn on him. I hope it doesn't drive us apart."

They are talking as though I am not in the room. Annoyed that I was ignored, I butted in so they would both realise

I was still in the room. "Margaret, let Fatima decide how and when. We all have a lot to think about. Let's leave it there for now."

We said goodbye courteously, not knowing if we would see Fatima again or want to. As we left, a thought dawned on me, so I asked Fatima, "How did you know we were here?"

"Mr Morris's feedback, some time ago."

"So, he is still employed by you to spy on Margaret?"

"Not really. He thought I should know you were making enquiries. He told me that you were digging for answers and were both very bright, that's all. So, I put the wheels in motion; border security checked your names on our system as 'people of interest'."

What was old Mr Morris playing at, crafty old bugger?

"Have you told him to stop, or will you tell him? Could you tell him that the dossier on Mum and me is mine?" Margaret instructed Fatima firmly. "Before it's too late."

"He looked like he was on his last legs to me," I added for extra urgency.

"Yes, of course, I will, and your names have also been wiped from our security systems."

We bade farewell again and left a forlorn Fatima waving goodbye to us.

In the limo on the way back to the hotel, Margaret kept repeating, "Surely he will want to see me, won't he?"

I kept replying, "Of course." But I was unsure.

A waiter placed a memo on our table the following day at breakfast, precisely as the day before. It was a different limo and driver this time. We asked the same question about where we were going, only to be told by the driver to wait and see. The limo pulled onto a concealed drive of a large townhouse. The driver got out, pointing to the large, ornate wooden door. He said, "Press the bell." He stayed sitting in the car.

The door opened, and standing grinning in the doorway was Emre, his arms outstretched as far as they could go, as you do when you greet a young child. Margaret flew into his arms; they wrapped around her, and her feet were off the ground.

I could hear Emre repeatedly whispering, "Sorry."

Once inside the house, he guided us into a reception room with Western-style furniture and asked us to sit. Emre repeated, "I am so sorry, I didn't know."

"No need to be sorry; you didn't know about me."

"But I should have. I should have gone back to find out why she wasn't responding to my letters. How could I have got it so wrong?"

"I am here now. I have dreamt of this moment all my life. I do have a daddy."

Emre turned and addressed me, "You are going to look after my child; let's not let history repeat itself."

"Of course, sir, if she will have me."

Margaret enquired, "Where is Fatima?"

"She has gone away for a bit."

"Oh, I hope you weren't too hard on her."

"She shouldn't have done what she did; it's going to be hard to forgive."

"She did ensure that I was looked after. I thought that was you."

"Yes, she did, but not for the right reasons, and it should have been me. Things would have been so different if she hadn't stopped your mother's letters."

"She told me you were working abroad on top secret stuff. Other than that, you were never mentioned."

Emre's eyes, full of tears, spoke reminiscently, "What threw me was you mentioned Barafundle Bay. That was our secret place."

"That's where I was conceived, wasn't it?"

A step too far; why does she jump in with both feet?

"Yes, it was." Tears were running down his cheeks; he turned and wiped them away. "Can you stay here with me, the both of you? If you want, we can learn more about each other."

"What do you think, Ali? Is that okay with you?"

"Fine by me."

"Okay, I will show you to your room."

Room? This will be interesting.

Emre led us into a large bedroom containing a large bed. Margaret glanced at me and smiled, saying, "This will do nicely."

"The beds can be pushed apart. I'll leave that up to you." Emre looked at me knowingly.

"We have no clothes or toiletries. Should I return to the hotel, collect them, and leave you two alone for a while?"

"If you could, that would be great. I'll instruct the driver."

My father's values came into my mind. How can it be two fathers the same age, born in the same country, and practising the same religion behave entirely differently? *I have lost a family because of this, and Margaret has gained a father.*

When I returned, it was clear what they had been doing in my absence. The table was covered in open letters. They were both sitting on a settee, side by side. Margaret's head leant onto her father's chest, his arm around her shoulder, comforting as a father does to his child. I could tell they had both been crying by the redness of their eyes. Emre pointed at a chair for me to sit, and Margaret raised her hand to acknowledge my return. I watched a father and daughter in silence, making up for the lost years. Were they thinking of what could have been? The loss of a mother and of a lover. Or the future?

We stayed with Emre for the few remaining days. Fatima didn't return; her absence wasn't mentioned. I watched the love between father and daughter develop. How strange that their charismatics were so similar.

Chapter 5

Back at Oxford, 1995

We returned to Oxford to continue our studies. I decided to continue renting my flat as it was the address the Syrian Army used for communication, though I never used it. I lived at Margarets' place full time.

When unpacking my stuff at Margaret's flat, she noticed some of my skipping ropes. Surprised, she asked, "Why have you got girls' skipping ropes?"

Puzzled, I replied, "For skipping, of course, and they're not just for girls."

"Skipping is for girls, not grown men."

"Have you tried it?"

"Only as a child. I am a grown-up now. I don't play with toys."

"Can you still skip?"

"It's like riding a bike; you never forget. I can still remember some of the songs we used to sing."

"I have two ropes. We can skip together then, and you can teach the songs."

"On your own, lovely. It's a children's game."

"Come on, give it a go?"

"Not in here."

"Of course not. Next time we go to the park, okay?"

"Only if there's no one watching."

"It's a good exercise; I am sure you'll enjoy it."

So the next time we went for a walk in the park, I put the ropes in our 'bits and pieces' bag we took everywhere, without Margaret noticing. When I pulled out the skipping ropes, Margaret uttered in disbelief, "I didn't mean it."

"Go on, give it a try. You don't have to sing."

Reluctantly tutting, she replied, "Okay, just this once; I hope no one is watching."

"Pease pudding hot, please pudding cold.
Pease pudding in the pot nine days old.
Some like it hot, some like it cold.
Some like it in the pot nine days old."

She sang along while skipping. She could skip a bit; the rope didn't always clear her feet, but she improved after a bit. She was pleased with her effort and laughed. "Your turn with the kiddie's rope. You don't have to sing."

Not to show off, I skipped the 'basic jump' and slowly increased the speed until the rope whistled. Margaret clapped, saying, "Very good for a kiddie." I increased the speed, then went through some of my repertoires; 'lateral jumps', 'half jacks', 'high knees running', 'the boxer step', and 'jump rope criss-cross'. "So that is where you get your physique. I knew it couldn't be swimming."

"I could teach you if you want?"

"No thanks, I'll stick to swimming."

"But it's out in the fresh air; it's so good for you."

"Ali, you are incredibly good at skipping. I am particularly good at swimming; let's leave it there."

We both studied hard, as Margaret's idea of helping each other in our studies worked well. She was a different Margaret since finding her father; she was always assertive, but now she was confident, too. I was now an orphan after my family had disowned me. Nothing could stop us from losing George's 'living for today' dogma now and committing to our future together. It made sense after graduation that we should make our home in Syria. Margaret would be close to her father, and I had to return to the army and complete my training. We had nothing keeping us in England except for a few friends; hopefully, we could visit now and then.

George invited us to an intercollege rugby match. It was my first, so I was unsure what to expect. A young lady accompanied George; we hadn't met before. She seemed pleasant enough. I got the impression from George that he wouldn't see her again. George didn't make a massive thing of the introduction of Vanessa, whom we never met again.

We met George in a local pub close to the match ground. Most of the crowd in the pub could be identified as students by the long colourful scarfs draped around their necks. George chose seats close to the field of play so we could get close to the action. It was one of those typical English windless spring days when the sun was bright and the sky blue, with just the odd fluffy white cloud. George declared the perfect weather for rugby.

George did a running commentary of what was happening on the field. I tried to indicate I understood, but I didn't. I could hardly hear his words because of the boos and cheers the students were shouting for no apparent reason I could understand. I thoroughly enjoyed the occasion but was unsure if it was a good match. The supporters of both teams seemed happy, regardless of who won. I wasn't sure of that either. George claimed it was a good game.

George insisted we pop into the clubhouse for a drink afterwards because the atmosphere would be good as both teams will be there; there should be lots of ribbing and banter.

I asked George, "Won't the fighting continue?"

"Fighting? There wasn't any fighting, just a few slight misunderstandings. They'll be buying each other pints. Wait and see."

"It looked like fighting to me."

George was correct; the opponents had arms around each other, and the banter was not taken seriously. Margaret was making fun of my girly skipping to George and Vanessa. Shouting over the raucous crowd milling at the bar, "Do you know that Ali has skipping ropes? He takes them to the park, hoping the other kiddies will join him."

George seemed interested and asked Margaret, "Is he any good at it?"

With her bemused expression, Margaret nodded and said, "He's okay. Why?"

George disappeared into the melee surrounding the bar. I thought he was fighting his way to the bar to buy another round of drinks. But he returned with one of the rugby players, introducing him as the captain and me as Ali, saying, "This bloke can skip; he knows all the moves."

The captain said, "Brilliant!" He held out his hand to shake mine. "Would you like to come to a training session?"

"Why, I know nothing about rugby?"

"We always look to do different things; training can get boring sometimes."

I agreed to attend a training session with my skipping ropes between George and the captain. So, I got 'roped' into the training session.

With a broad smile, the team coach introduced me as an international expert in skipping in front of the players. There was a lot of 'mickey-taking'.

One player asked, "Can I bring my little sister?"

Another one asked me, "Are you any good at hopscotch?"

Another butted in; he stood about two metres tall with a barrel chest which didn't taper at his waistline. He stood on legs wider than my chest, with similarly massive arms that seemed inflexible. "What about playing marbles?" he said, directed at a similar proportioned player.

With a threatening look, he replied, "You lost your marbles in the scrum last week."

The two giants faced each other, forehead to forehead, before the coach said, "Come on, girls, I wish you showed your opponents the same aggression; perhaps we would have a chance of winning our put-in." Then, he added, after the head-butting contest stopped, "All right, stop the piss-taking; Ali has gone out of his way to show you something. Show some bloody respect. He's here to improve your foot speed and burn off the ten pints you shoved down your gullet after the last game you lost."

I could see the player's body language change; last week's loss must have affected them. They became less opposed to the idea of trying skipping.

George had mentioned the last game was a derby match. I wasn't sure what it meant, but it seemed significant to the players waiting for me to show them my skipping moves. So, nervously, I showed about half the team basic skipping. The coach called them forwards. Surprisingly, the size of the players didn't affect their ability to skip as much as I thought it would.

The coach called the other half of the team over from the other side of the field by blowing his whistle and calling out, "Sprint!" They had a similar physique to me. They arrived hardly out of breath and seemed far less aggressive than the forwards. The coach addressed them as 'backs'. Unsurprisingly, most could learn the basics quicker than the forwards.

After a few minutes of skipping, one of the backs complained, "What's the point? I'm hardly out of breath."

I knew from my army training that I had to start slowly and build speed to not leave anyone behind. "Okay, that's the basic stuff," I told the complainer. I added, "Why not try this." I raised my speed and made the rope whistle. I watched as they tried and failed to get near my pace as the ropes became entangled in their feet. I stopped skipping and said, "This is not showing off. Just showing you a few steps that took years of practice to perfect."

The coach addressed the backs and me, saying, "We can all learn from other sports, Ali. I could see you were holding back. You've not broken into a sweat; show them what you can do." So, I did my entire repertoire, not holding back until the coach stopped me, saying, "That's enough; we've homes to go to."

The players clapped, and one said, "Shit, you're good."

The other half of the team was at the other end of the field. They seemed to be either wrestling with each other or pushing heavy sledges across the turf.

The coach said, "You're fit. Is it just the skipping?"

"Mostly, but I used to do a lot of wrestling in Syria."

"You any good at it?"

"I used to be okay. I used to skip to build up my reflexes and stamina."

I was intrigued watching the game on Saturday, as the front players in the scrum were wrestling with each other. So, I asked the coach, "Could I have a go at wrestling in the scrum."

He looked at me and laughed. "You're too small, too light."

"I am stronger than I look, and the technique counts, right?"

Still smiling, he shouted, "Hey, Bill, do us a favour and get Alfie from the youth team."

Bill returned with a young boy, about 16 years old, at a guess. The coach introduced me to Alfie, saying, "This is Ali; he thinks he's a prop. Do you want you to show him what it's all about?"

Alfie laughed. "You're having me on? He's no prop."

"Alfie, he wants a try. Be gentle with him."

Alf grinned, saying, "Okay, but don't blame me if he gets hurt."

So, the coach positioned us with our shoulders locked against each other and said, "Don't either of you push; just take each other's weight and push when I say so."

I waited for the coach to say push, and as soon as the word 'push' was uttered, I was driven backwards ten meters.

Alfie told the coach, "I told you so."

Embarrassed and shocked, I said, "I wasn't ready. Can we try again?"

Alfie said, "To be fair, he wasn't wearing boots, not that it'll make a difference."

The coach said, "Fair comment, Alfie." The coach took his boots off and told me, "Put them on and try again."

"Bloody hell, coach, they won't make any difference. I wasn't trying that much."

So, I got my way, and the coach set us up again. This time, I was determined not to budge. When the coach said push, I expected to do better but was driven back even harder.

Alfie looked pleased he was right, telling the coach, "He looks like a girly back to me; he'd be better hanging around with them."

The coach added, "See, you are not a prop; too small to be any forward. Can you throw, catch a ball, or run?

"I haven't tried with a rugby ball, but I can run okay."

"Twice a week we train, every Tuesday and Thursday if you are interested. Bring your skipping ropes if you want."

That was my introduction to rugby. I did learn how to catch and pass the ball. The game's rules seemed complicated as a spectator began to make sense. Eventually, I was picked for the seconds as an inside centre. My wrestling skills were helpful at the breakdowns. I was selected as a replacement for the first on a few occasions.

Chapter 6
Antalya, Ali Recovering, 2014

Warm breath on my face, something tickling my cheek, *dangling hair?*

Can I smell the scent of Margaret?

Is she here?

Are we on this journey together?

Am I blind? I repeatedly frantically whispered, "Ali Mansour."

I can hear muffled noises; *people talking?*

Am I in Limbo?

Are they checking my name against a list?

I shouldn't be on this journey.

Is it a mistake?

Am I unworthy as a non-believer?

Perhaps they are deciding where I should go.

Is there another place?

A finger? Tracked down my forehead onto my nose and lips.

It's Margaret's touch. She often did that.

Then, her other hand gently squeezed mine.

Why couldn't I squeeze back?

Something is removed from my face; it's no longer night.

Dusk maybe? I can see ghostly white shapes moving around me.

Have I reached my destination?

Muffled sounds, gentle hands. *Female?* Fiddling with something on my head.

Then a tingling sensation feels like sticky tape removed, hairs gently pulled. I close my eyes; the light is too bright.

Squinting, I focus on the *white ghosts?* Moving around me, they slowly become visible.

People in white coats?

Strange things to wear in this place.

Then a face appears close to mine; it's Margaret's, her eyes filled with tears as kohl lines run down her cheeks.

Is she really here, too?

Why is she crying?

Perhaps we are going to different places.

She looks older now, not as in my dreams.

Is she smiling?

Are the tears of joy?

Margaret is talking, looking at me, and wiping her eyes. I hear her muffled voice.

What's she saying?

A white coat approaches me, carrying headphones.

Headphones?

Do they use them in this place?

Why can't I move?

I'm trembling in anticipation like before.

I thought my pain had ended with death.

"No, no, please, no," I am screaming.

Why doesn't he stop?

Can't he hear me?

Headphones are gently placed around my head and carefully adjusted to fit comfortably.

Adept, solid and firm but not rough?
A man's hand?
No slapping or punching?
I am not tightly strapped to a chair as before.
Is it different in this place?

I expected to hear the recorded excruciating screams of tortured men, women, and children and me screaming my name. Then, the volume would increase until my head felt like it was about to explode. Then the pain would increase till I lost consciousness like before in Raqqa.

Instead, just a faint buzzing noise, then silence.

This is different.
Strange, this has never happened before.
What are they going to do next?

Margaret's face is close to mine.

Her voice trembles. "If you can hear me, blink your eyes."

I wasn't hallucinating she was here, or was this a dream within a dream?
She looks anxious.
My throat is sore and dry.

I blink and feebly croak, "Are you really here? It is you?"

One of the 'white coats' approaches, and water droplets enter my mouth.

"Yes, Ali, it is me; you are safe now."

So, we are on our journey together?

"Are you coming with me then? It's not a dream?"

"We are together now. You're not going anywhere."

Together?
Where?

"Where am I?"

"Antalya"

I want more water so I don't croak.

"More water, please."

That's better.

"Antalya, Turkey?"

"Yes, Ali."

"Why Antalya?"

"You're in a hospital, receiving treatment, doing well."

What is wrong with me? I can't move, yet I can see, hear, and talk?

"I thought I was going to the other place and you were coming with me."

"You are alive and getting the best care possible, but it will take time."

Is this true?

Am I alive?

"Why can't I move?"

"The doctors induced you to a deep sleep so your injuries could be treated easier."

Only a few moments ago, I was in Raqqa. I was floating to the other place, amongst my dreams of Margaret.

What injuries?

"Wasn't that just a few moments ago?"

"No, darling, you have been here a long time. I have been beside you for most of it. I thought you would sense me."

Coma? I have been in a coma.

"How long have I been in a coma?"

"Weeks. I arrived a couple of days after you arrived here."

"I thought it was a dream; I could smell you."
"I hoped you would. I wore your favourite perfume."
"Opium?"
"Yes, Opium."
"You couldn't see or hear; I hoped you could still smell."

Margaret kissed my cheek. "That's enough talking, for now, time to rest."

"What injuries?"

The white coats moved closer…

Was Margaret here?

Am I being tested?

I am awake. The white coats move around me quickly. The bed backboard is raised slowly. I am being observed: a white coat moves closer. My eyelids are gently pulled and held open quickly, one at a time.

A female hand?

A light briefly flashes in front of my eyes. Something is gently inserted into my ears, left, then right.

I hear noises of *rustling paper? Muffled voices?*

I observe a white coat remove a chart from the end of the bed. Another white coat gently fiddles with something in my ears.

The sounds are audible now, with no buzzing noise.

She notices I am looking at her, smiles and speaks. "Günaydin."

Assessing my hearing?

I know a little Turkish, so I whisper, "Günaydin."

My voice has a lisp. *Strange.*

I run my tongue around my mouth.

Something isn't right. Gaps in my teeth; what has happened?

"Sabah al-kheir." I turn to my left; Margaret sits beside my bed, smiling.

She is here?

"Good morning to you, too," I reply in return.

Margaret sits on my bed, nodding her head. She looks pleased. "You're back, inshallah."

Where have I been?

What has happened to me?

"Back from where?"

"There is plenty of time for that. Getting you back is the main thing."

I fall asleep again, sitting up...

A loud American voice awakes me. "Sergeant Wayne Brantley, ma'am. Is it okay to visit your husband?"

"Do you know Ali, then?"

"No, not really, ma'am."

"So why are you here?"

"I found him, ma'am, in Raqqa prison.

"So, were you involved in his recovery then?"

"Yes, ma'am"

"Thank God you found him in time."

"The YPJ and YPG deserve all the credit, ma'am. We only came in at the end when the fighting was all over. Searching the toilet block for survivors, many were discarded to die. We were collecting the poor souls that didn't survive and body-bagging them. Your husband was curled up in the foetal position. When I touched him, he feebly whispered, 'Ali Mansour'. I called over a medic, and we gently lifted him onto a stretcher."

Floating? Solid arms? Could they be his?

My eyes opened. I could see a youngish, large, broad, athletic man dressed in an American desert camouflage uniform. His legs were wide apart, *at ease?* He has his hands behind his back, *possibly holding his cap?*

Margaret inquired, "What happened next?"

"I contacted Rojda Felat, the operation's YPJ commander, that evening with my report. She was extremely interested when I mentioned Ali Mansour as one of those rescued. She asked if he was okay, so I told her he needed urgent medical attention. She ordered, 'Ensure that is done, Sergeant, because I have a good friend called Ali Mansour; it could be him.' So, ma'am, that's what I am doing here, checking him out as ordered."

The name of my friend, Rojda Felat, jolted me fully awake. I coughed to clear my throat, to ensure they knew I was listening to their conversation.

I could sense concern in Margaret's voice as she spoke. "Sergeant, it appears that Ali is awake."

Margaret raised the back of my bed so I could see them both. "Thanks, Margaret. Rojda Felat, a commander in the YPJ. She is a good friend of mine," I squeaked.

Wayne clicked his heels together, stood to attention, and saluted me. "Sir, I have a message from Rojda Felat to provide you with anything you require."

"A single malt Scotch whisky would do."

"I wish," Wayne replied, adding, "maybe next time."

"Stand at ease, Sergeant. I am no longer in the army."

"I know that sir, but the order from Rojda Felat was to show respect to a fellow officer."

"That is a lovely gesture, but please stand at ease, Sergeant," Margaret said, pointing to a chair.

"Could you thank Rojda for helping my good friend, Allan James, and his family to escape safely when you report back to her?"

The sergeant, still standing, said, "No problem, sir."

After a pause, Wayne said, "They are a lovely family; I helped them on their journey a little while back."

Margaret interrupted, "You helped them? Where and when?

"I took them across the Syrian border to Kirikhan, Turkey, ma'am."

Margaret nodded, saying, "Yes, they are lovely and our best friends."

Wayne, still standing, replied, "Did they all get to the UK safely, then?"

Margaret nodded, and I said, "Yes, thanks to you and the YPJ."

Margaret added, "They were all doing well the last time we spoke. They did mention an American sergeant and the YPJ with great affection."

After a short pause, I said, "Thank you, Sergeant. Can I shake your hand for going the extra yard?"

Wayne moved closer with his arm outstretched; I tried to move my hand towards his, but nothing happened. Wayne put his hand on the back of mine and shook it gently, saying, "It's okay, buddy, I've got it." Margaret stood on tiptoes, embraced Wayne, and whispered in his ear. Wayne smiled and said, "There is no need, but thank you, ma'am, all the same." He then looked at me and said, "Get well, buddy." As he left, he casually saluted, adding, "Would a Jack Daniels be okay?"

Margaret, smiling, said, "It's a small world; who would have thought it?"

"Why can't I move my arms?"

"They're not strong enough yet; it will take longer. You have come a long way already."

"Could you raise the headboard slightly more so I can see better?"

Margaret pressed a few buttons on the bed handset, and I could see around the small room. There was another bed touching mine; *strange*. I could see my hands were bandaged, and cannulas were poking through the bandage. The bed sheets couldn't hide that my arms, legs, and torso were thin, just skin and bone. *That is why I can't move.*

"Could you get me a mirror, Margaret?"

"Why?"

There's something not right about my mouth."

"Maybe later, darling; it's not time for that yet."

"Do I look that bad? What are you trying to hide?"

"Ali, seeing what has been done to you will only make you angry; it will only be a short time before you look better, okay?

She kissed my cheek and said, "Get some sleep. You will be better for it."

I awoke and turned to where Margaret was sitting; the chair was empty. I turned to the right, and on the other bed, Margaret was fast asleep. A nurse, realising I was awake, approached close to my bed and quietly asked, "Can I get you anything?"

"Water, please." As the nurse poured the water, I asked quietly, "How long has Margaret been sleeping beside me?"

"Since you got here, she has always been here."

"How long has that been?"

"I don't know exactly, maybe six weeks."

"Six weeks?"

"Yes, she was poorly when she first arrived – malnutrition – so we thought it best for you to be close."

"Malnutrition?"

"Yes, it's been hell in Aleppo; people are starving to death."

"Is she okay now? She looks tired."

"She's fine; it's been hard, but she is getting there."

"So, I have been out of it most of the time?"

"Yes, mostly. You come to, then drop off to sleep occasionally."

"Like yesterday, you mean?"

"Why yesterday?"

"I dropped off to sleep just after the American sergeant left."

"That wasn't yesterday."

"It was. I can remember it clearly."

"Mr Mansour, the soldier visited over a week ago."

Oh no, what is happening to me?

. . . . .

Whistling cluster bombs, incendiaries, mortars, rockets, and barrel bombs, I never knew which until they landed; the destruction confirmed which. Deafening thuds, explosions, men, women, babes in arms, and children running, screaming, unsure if they were running into cover or danger. The ground shook, flashes of red, yellow, and orange, the smell of explosives burning wood and flesh. Debris, stones, iron, wood, and steel flew through the air in all directions. Thick dust and black and grey putrid smoke filled the air, my eyes stinging, I couldn't see. The air cleared, buildings, where people fled were no longer there. At first, they were almost silent. The only noise was crumbling masonry toppling onto the piles in the eerie silence. I was wheezing; the force of the explosion sucked the air from my lungs. Gasping for breath, confused about where to search. Slowly, desperate screams emitted from beneath the rubble. Men like me in white helmets ran to the heaps of debris where buildings once stood.

Listening for sounds, digging with bare hands, shovels, and iron bars, stopping to listen. Locating where the cries were coming from. There was no time to talk, hands raised, screaming, "Be quiet!" Trying to find where the sound came from. Shouting, pointing 'over here'. If help was needed to hear a whine or whimper. Slowly, mechanical diggers would arrive, trained sniffer dogs on leads. Working, sweating, limbs aching, exhausted, unable to rest, people joining, knowing what the consequences might be as we waited for the 'second tap'. We knew we were being watched from the sky. The watchers knew precisely when the 'second tap' could do the most damage, so we were always alert for the next whistle.

Not many poor souls pulled from the wrecked buildings were alive. Tiny arms and legs, once reached, confirmed that children are the least likely to survive. Injured who required urgent medical treatment were loaded onto ambulances or trucks. Survivors with the strength to help join us in frantically searching, hoping to find family, friends, or anyone alive. Others kneeled, heads on the ground, some praising Allah, others accusing him. Some were shaking, unable to stand; others sat with glazed eyes. Uncontrollable crying would start soon, followed by rage against those who caused this and Allah, who didn't stop it. The dead were body-bagged and placed onto different trucks. Mechanical diggers travelled behind to bury them without time for the ceremony. When almost all we could do was done, came the 'second tap' targeting the rescuers, survivors, injured, ambulances and the already dead. Ambulances were targeted again if they reached the hospitals. This was not war, one army pitting its might against another. This war was against innocents. The aim was to obliterate everything, so nothing was worth fighting for. The mass exodus continued at a greater pace, leaving the destroyed buildings and the stench of rotting corpses to the victor...

Are they talking about me?

"He is having another one of his turns again; his eyes are moving frantically from side to side."

Another voice, a man's this time. "This will help." Something touches my arm...

I am so tired; I need a few hours of sleep, a shower, and clean clothes, but the bombardments are endless. Survivors are moving away to find places of safety, carrying all they have left the best way they can. Fewer survivors now mixed among the rebel fighters, the real target of the government forces. It's days since I last saw Margaret.

Voices again?

"See, he's more settled now."

Someone shouts, "Ali Mansour!"

I turn; who is it? I know that face. I remember he was in the army, too.

"Hi, Mohammed. How are you?"

"Fine, what's with the white helmet?" He spat back with a puzzled look.

He was carrying a rifle and ammunition belts crisscrossed across his chest. Not in army uniform; a rebel fighter?

He had always looked scruffy in an army uniform; nothing had changed. I recall an argument we had about religion. His views were very radical, not liberal, like mine. I used to be of higher rank, but that didn't help in controlling him.

He repeats again, "What's with the white helmet?

"Just trying to help these poor people."

"There are infidels. You should leave them to rot."

"No, they are human beings; we don't check what religion, if any, or what side of the war they were on. We don't discriminate. I would even save you."

Mohammed was now standing face-to-face with me. He was a small, scrawny man who always smelled of lousy breath and stale sweat. I reprimanded him a few times for his unsatisfactory appearance. Nothing had changed, except his aroma was even worse. I tried to walk away, but he grimaced through brown tea-stained teeth and issued an order as though he had command over me. "Standstill until I tell you to move."

Exhausted, I couldn't be bothered by his infantile attitude. From previous experience, we both knew he would have no chance if it came to a hand fight. So, I shrugged my shoulders in indifference, turned and walked away. After a few steps, he whacked my head with the butt of his rifle, shouting, "Did I say you could go?"

It hurt, but I didn't go down but turned to confront him. His rifle pointed towards my stomach. I was just about to knock the gun away when more fighters appeared. I am confident I could have disarmed Mohammed, but not a small group of armed rebels. So, I resisted the temptation to change the colour of his teeth from brown to red. I heard Mohammed tell them I used to be his commanding officer and was not a good Muslim. Also, I had a non-Muslim wife, and I drank alcohol...

Margaret wakes me, gently rocking my shoulder while placing an ice-cold pack on my forehead. Then the bed is raised, I feel her hand under my chin, and a glass of water is placed on my bottom lip. "It's okay," she repeats repeatedly as she strokes my arm...

Chapter 7

Moving to Syria, 1996

With Emre's help and many discussions, we all agreed that it made sense that Margaret had nothing to keep her in the UK. Her father lived in Syria, and I would be compelled to return soon. Our 'living for today' pledge dispersed as we planned to spend the rest of our lives together.

Emre's influence as a government minister allowed him to find me a position as an intelligence officer in the Syrian Army. The role was like a nine-to-five job, which suited our circumstances. The task was important, not contrived, as the government was aware of the insurgence of rebelling citizens and foreign nationals who could harm the oil industry.

Finding Margaret an appointment at a university was easy because her knowledge base was ideal, being schooled in Arabic history and language. However, she had to change her dress and attitude. And not be as forward as she would have liked.

Our marriage arrangements were made mainly by Emre. Though Margaret did the finer details. This enabled us to be married swiftly. There was only one minor condition outside our small group, including

Fatima. No one else should be told that Emre was Margaret's father for fear that religious zealots opposed to Emre's more modern stance could use it against him. As could anyone ambitious seeking to remove him from his role as a minister.

The wedding was small and informal, just the four of us. There was no point telling my parents of the marriage, as it would only compound their belief that I had lost my way and become unclean. Emre hadn't forgiven Fatima for her deceit. To her credit, she had accepted his infidelity, and they were cordial to each other. Both Margaret and I believed that one day, they would rekindle the love they once had. As far as we know, neither of them had anyone else in their lives.

We rented an apartment close to Aleppo and within reasonable distance for work. Our workloads were relatively low, which enabled us to spend more time with each other, like a normal married couple.

I had plenty of spare time on my hands. Observing lazy workers and avoiding ex-pat employees was mainly dull. It seemed that they took more effort to avoid work than do it. I organised hidden security cameras installed to monitor and record all the site activity. Installing them within the fire detection system meant we had complete site surveillance. All security came under my control, so it was easy to ensure its installation was done without detection by the ex-pat workforce. I could see and hear everything, even inside the accommodation blocks from the security control room. There was no privacy, and everything could be watched – well, almost everything. Thankfully, there were no fire alarm detectors in the bathrooms.

There was nothing much to do until a new employer, Allan James, arrived as the maintenance planner. The ex-pat worker's habits of avoiding work fitted a predictive pattern. I was bored watching them. They must have been just as bored as me; they put more ingenuity into doing nothing than it would do to do the work.

"Get off your arse and do something," I muttered frustratedly.

Then, things changed and became interesting when I observed Allan James in the planning department. From the outset, he didn't seem like the others, which caused tension with the superintendents. Instead of skiving, Allan James was intent on installing the maintenance system he was employed to. Bente, the chief superintendent, opposed this and insisted things remain the same. I could see the confusion on Allan's face when Bente insisted he didn't want him to do what he was recruited to do. Bente demanded that Allan not install the maintenance programme supplied. Instead, he was instructed to fabricate bogus wall charts and planning schedules to confirm the current work was on schedule. The discussions were quite lively and amusing as a voyeur. Allan was left with no alternative but reluctantly carry out Bente's instructions. Allan always won the arguments between them. It became apparent to me that Bente was either completely incompetent or corrupt.

After heated arguments, when Bente left his office, Allan often told the empty room what he thought of Bente. He used choice Anglo-Saxon swear words – most I had heard at Oxford, but some were new to me. Bente was a tall, well-built man who used his physical presence to try and intimidate Allan. On one occasion, Bente came storming into the planning office. Standing red-faced, he yelled, nose to nose with Allan, "Are you putting it around that I am going around the twist?"

Allan responded immediately, "Why, is it a secret?"

Bente's face was a picture of confusion; unable to respond, he turned and left the room, uttering, "You're finished." He slammed the door shut.

Allan uttered, "Prick." Bente may have heard the comment as he paused slightly before storming off.

I couldn't help laughing out loud as it confirmed what I believed was the case. Bente was not up to the job; regardless of his mental ability, he was dishonest and a prick.

Allan uncovered many things that couldn't be explained and confronted Bente at every opportunity. All that he got back from Bente was bluster, unable to sway Allan to his thinking. Their differences were always left unresolved. The big issue with Allan was the revenue budget. I watched as he cornered Bente, asking for an explanation of where the money budgeted for was going as little work on that budget was conducted. Bente replied that it was none of his business and to do as he was told, which was his answer for everything.

Getting to know Emre, I realised how unlike my father he was. My father would also listen to and support me as a child. As I matured and questioned my father, his mind became a locked door. No amount of discussion would change his concept of what was right or wrong. It was my father's way; he was always right. To disagree was to disobey, and the consequences would be a punishment. Whereas Emre was open to debate. Maybe because of his education and travel to different lands, his mind was open to other concepts. He was like George in many ways. We could talk all night and disagree agreeably as friends, both of us gaining something from the debate. So, when I was not on duty, Emre often was a guest at our apartment in Aleppo, or we were at his house in Damascus.

During one of our visits to Emre's house, I mentioned the arguments between Allan James and Bente regarding the lack of maintenance at the refineries and the mystery of how the budgets were spent. Emre was engrossed by what I told him and requested a copy of the security CCTV tapes. We often watched the recordings together. It became a sort of light entertainment for us watching Allan run rings around Bente. Though the interaction between Bente and Allan was amusing, it was also deadly serious. Emre decided the corruption must end, so he arranged an official visit under the guise that he was interested in the efficiency of the refineries run by overseas labour.

The visit went as planned, and he had a guided tour of the refineries, including a visit to the planning office, where he was introduced to a sheepish Allan James, who looked embarrassed. The visit confirmed things were not as they should have been. Emre couldn't believe that the childish bar charts and graphs on the walls proved anything other than it was farcical. The planning office should have a team of planning engineers. Instead, one person verified that the work was conducted and signed off entirely by the same hand, an impossible task. Emre described Bente as a 'prick', agreeing with the term Allan had used to describe him. I had picked up the word in the UK. It is a pejorative term, so the description was accurate as he was despicable and contemptible, confirmed by my daily observations of him at the pointless morning communication meetings.

Shortly after Emre's visit, several ex-pat workers and a Syrian driver went missing. The security team searched the local roads and found no trace of them or the vehicle they were using. To begin with, my first conclusion was they had broken down or were lost. The Syrian driver was familiar with the area and trained to stay with the vehicle if either of those events occurred.

The vehicle was not equipped to go off-road, so if it wasn't on local roads, it was either no longer in the area or well hidden. There were a few travelling Bedouin tribes in the area as it was the harvesting season. The women and children worked in the fields in scorching weather – backbreaking work for so little wage. So, one option was they might have been taken captive. Money was the most likely motive, as it's a hard life being a Bedouin, even for the men who did little work.

If the well-dressed, opulent foreigners wandered into the wrong area, perhaps some enterprising Bedouin seized an opportunity to exploit the situation. So, I notified all the regional banks regarding attempted cash withdrawals from the named accounts of those missing. I also set up surveillance at the banks as money was the likely motive. The cash machines would be the less chancy method to obtain it. As it turned out, my assumption was correct. The following night, a truck stopped a couple of hundred metres from one of the banks under surveillance – obviously a Bedouin vehicle by its state and the faded, typically elaborate artwork. After 10 minutes, four men gingerly got out of the truck.

The driver stayed with the truck, furtively looking in all directions. The blue tailpipe smoke indicated the engine was running and not well maintained. Two Bedouins positioned themselves opposite the bank, looking furtively in all directions. The remaining Bedouin crossed the road and then turned to check with the other three before standing in front of the ATM. He took ages, continually turning to get the all-clear from the lookouts. I was unable to see clearly why he was taking so much time. *Perhaps the bank cards were written in the English language. He wouldn't be familiar with that.* He turned and walked at pace back to the truck. The other Bedouins were already waiting for his return. I had four surveillance vehicles with radio communications in the area. We took turns following them at a distance so as not to raise suspicion. The Bedouin truck eventually turned off the road into a Bedouin camp. One of our vehicles parked some distance away to observe the campsite.

The following day, I flew drones over the Bedouin camp to establish if the missing workers were still there. We discovered they were still being held as prisoners in different tents, some distance apart, made evident by armed guards stationed outside each tent.

I decided night would be the best time to launch a rescue. We could cause more confusion at night. Most of the Bedouins would be asleep, possibly the guards too. The light from a crescent moon would make it difficult for them to see us, but we could see them clearly through our night vision goggles. From my observations, I decided that Allan James would be my target; from my spying on him, I considered I knew him and considered him more worthy of saving. I was unsure about the other three as they were from a different refinery.

The drones were set to night vision; we knew precisely where the hostages were because our drones observed them abluting during the day. Allan was lying with his torso outside the tent. He appeared to be preoccupied, eyes open, watching the magnificent night sky, possibly pondering the meaning of life. I jumped onto him and forced my hand over his mouth. Surprisingly, he didn't seem to have any strength and was easy to pin down. After about a minute, I could feel all his resistance disappear. I had to be careful not to suffocate him. I whispered in his ear, "When you hear a bang, run to the road." I disabled the guard at the front of the tent. It wasn't hard as he was fast asleep; one swift blow to his temple with the butt of my gun. As the saying goes, 'he never knew what hit him'. I ran into the centre of the camp. I gave a sharp blast on my whistle. Flares were fired into the night sky, exploding with three loud bangs as planned. They descended slowly, dropping to the ground and illuminating the campsite in bright white light. We had about two minutes before the darkness fell. One of my soldiers screamed into a Tannoy to surrender to cause even more confusion.

Now almost pitch black, it was to our advantage. Our night vision goggles allowed us to see the mayhem of panicked Bedouins who ran from their tents, confused by the bright white light, then thrown into utter darkness, making it easy to round them up. The three hostages seemed confused, wobbly on their feet, possibly drugged. They had to be helped – almost carried – by a soldier on either side of the highway, joining Allan James to be loaded onto the transport.

I decided that two males and four females involved with the hostages would be appropriate. Arresting any more than that wasn't an option. So we rounded up the suspects and handcuffed them.

Chapter 8
Allan James, 1996

Interrogating the four idiots who managed to get themselves captured was straightforward. It was down to one particular individual, Douglas Hitchins, and his strong Geordie accent and phrases, which became more difficult to decipher when challenged. He became overexcited and used unpronounceable words. He looked at me as though I was stupid and repeated the exact inaudible words. He appeared to grasp the gravity of his actions and was undoubtedly responsible for the event. Allan James, Matt Hamilton, and Mohammed's recollections of events were consistent with each other's accounts. They all confirmed it was Doug Hitchins who caused all the problems. Various descriptions included 'a right prat', 'a bampot' and 'a bloody maniac'. These were compatible with my conclusions; he was a majnun (madman).

During Allan James' interview, he appeared confused, perhaps as I was dressed in the uniform of a captain in the Syrian Army. At the morning communications meetings, I often saw him give me a quizzical look; maybe he didn't see the point in me being there as I contributed nothing. The other expats didn't seem that inquisitive; I often wondered why.

Seeing me in uniform must have filled his head with many questions. I had to point out that I was interviewing him, not vice versa. But I could tell he was troubled by my uniform, which made him reluctant to answer my questions without long pauses of contemplation. Like George and Emre, who contemplated before speaking, I liked that it proved he listened and was no one's fool. I avoided his question about the anomaly of my role by reminding him I was interviewing him.

After the debrief over the Bedouin incident, I turned my attention to his role as the maintenance planner, which, from my observations, he was not at ease with. So, after the interview, I adopted a more conciliatory tone, asked him about his role, and compared his answers to my observations. I could see that Allan was having difficulties giving accurate answers. Instead, his replies were well thought out without denying that he was entirely unhappy. I admired him for this; it persuaded me to ask more questions. To make things easier for Allan to accept my prying, I removed my uniform jacket, saying at the same time, "Please address me as Ali." He seemed hesitant, so I asked if he would like tea. Allan questioned me on my English; though excellent in his opinion, it had a slight London twang. I explained I went to uni at Oxford; perhaps that was why. It was probably the influence of my wife, Margaret, whom I had no intention of disclosing to him or anyone else.

Slowly, Allan became at ease; I thought maybe he was beginning to trust me a little. I realised that Allan was intelligent and not impulsive, and it would take time to earn his trust. I was fortunate that I had been able to witness his behaviour for a while, but he had only just met me. So, suggesting we became more open and friendly might seem odd to him. I realised I would have to build his trust in me, so I trod carefully, hoping he would recognise my good intentions.

He asked me what would happen to the Bedouins and wasn't happy when I told him there would be a trial and the punishment would be severe. Allan mentioned being befriended by a young Bedouin woman who cared for him. She told him in English she wasn't a Bedouin but Syrian, and her name was Amina. It was customary for young girls to be kidnapped by Bedouins, so I told Allan I would find out about her during her interrogation.

I had missed talking in English to another man casually. In a way, Allan reminded me of George. I missed the open and frank conversations with George. So, I asked if he would like to continue the conversation in my room, something I had never asked any of my army buddies. Allan was startled but tentatively accepted my offer out of curiosity or maybe a break from the tedium of inventing boring wall charts.

Allan was surprised with my comfortable accommodation compared to his and that I enjoyed a glass of Scotch whisky. I tried tentatively to direct the conversation to what he knew was happening at the refineries. Allan would give little away. I admired him for this as it is precisely what I would have done in his circumstances. I saw how difficult it was for him at work and could understand why he remained silent, as he still wasn't sure of my intentions.

Allan seemed more interested in what would become of the Bedouins, particularly the one he knew as Amina. He repetitively explained she had helped him, was not like the others, could speak a little English, and seemed to care about what was happening to him. I thought he was a little bit obsessed with her.

The Bedouins were individually interviewed, and I left Amina till last. Allan was correct; she was nothing like the rest of them. She was slight in build and didn't have the same facial characteristics as the others. I asked questions in English, and she had to be coaxed to answer as though it was a trap. When she did, it was evident that she had an adequate basic knowledge of the English language. I asked who taught her.

"Baba," was her reply.

She then gave me the full name of her mother and father and where they once lived. I noticed that she had a beautiful, delicate face with dark, expressive eyes, which were glassy with tears *in anticipation of the punishment she was about to receive?*

I wasn't entirely sure her story was true or that she had been kidnapped as a child. The Bedouins called her Habiba, but she told me her real name was Amina Yassin at the interview.

Allan became a regular visitor to my room, and like George, we talked about a wide range of things. Allan's confidence grew, and our conversations were far more relaxed. Allan continually manoeuvred the discussion to the likely outcome for Amina. His interest in Amina continued to be a little obsessive to me. Allan urged me to confirm Amina's story about her parents was true and find them. I informed him I would be doing that as a matter of course, and he should trust me to do my job correctly. It further confirmed to me that Allan was overly concerned about Amina.

Allan told me about his life history, marriage, children, divorce, and birthplace. I confided in him the issue with my parents, but not the real reason for my bust-up. I never disclosed my marriage to anyone other than on official documents. My private life was sacrosanct. Margaret and especially Emre would always be a secret. It had to be for Emre's sake.

In a further interview with Amina, she explained her reason for not attempting an escape. She was a child when she was told the Bedouins knew precisely where her parents lived. Her punishment, if caught, would be execution by sword, and her head would be placed on her parents' doorstep. If she wasn't recaptured and made it home, she would find her parents' heads on spikes outside their house. So, it must have been terrifying for her.

I received the report from Damascus regarding Amina's parents. The information Amina gave me was genuine. They were still living at the same address in Damascus. Everything checked out, including their names, occupation, and a reported missing daughter called Amina. Yoran and Souzan Yassin were likely to be the parents of Amina. So, the following weekend, while visiting Emre in Damascus, I decided to check them out personally and confirm they had a missing daughter, Amina.

I discussed the Bedouin event with Emre as I thought he might be interested in the mess the expat workers had gotten themselves into. When I mentioned the names of Amina's parents and where they lived, Emre inquisitively asked, "Is Yoran a doctor?"

Startled that Emre knew he was a doctor, I quizzically asked, "How do you know that?"

"Well, I have old friends by that name, and they had a daughter called Amina."

"Do you know if their daughter is still with them?"

"No, she isn't. She went missing some years ago, very sad, such a bright and pretty girl."

"I have a bit of a dilemma, as I am unsure what their reactions would be if their daughter was returned to them."

"In what way?"

"Would they welcome her back regardless of anything that could have happened to her without spelling it out? I think you know what I mean."

"From what I remember of them – it has been a few years – I think they would be delighted. I know what it's like to find a child you didn't know you had but to have one returned you thought was lost? That excitement would be on a higher level."

"That's a relief. I have an idea. Why don't we visit them together?"

"I would love to see them again. Souzan is a natural beauty; Yoran snapped her up before I had a chance," Emre replied whimsically.

"So that's settled then. You and I are house-calling tomorrow, okay?"

"Fine, now tell me about the Bedouin incident."

"Well, stupidly, four of the workers got taken hostage by the Bedouins; it was all down to one person. But you will probably be surprised that the bloke on the tapes I sent you is one of them."

"You mean the planner?"

"Yes, him."

"Well, I thought others could do something that stupid, but the planner seemed to have some common sense."

"Yeah, but he unwittingly got caught up in it. I have been unofficially chatting with the planner, trying to find the truth about what's happening at the refinery. Is that okay?"

"Yes, fine; from what I have seen on the security tapes, he seems trustworthy."

"I think he has taken a fancy to Amina; she looked after him on the Bedouin campsite."

"If she is anything like her mother, I don't blame him."

"From what you have said, she is."

So, the following day, we went to visit the Yassins unannounced. We decided how we would approach the situation without building up their hope and how to ensure the return of Amina if, in fact, she was their daughter was the right thing for them. Luckily, they were both at home, which we expected as it was the weekend.

Yoran was surprised to find Emre on their doorstep, recognising him almost immediately. Even though it had been a while since they last met, he seemed puzzled why Emre was on their doorstep accompanied by me. "Please come in," he said. He turned and, raising his voice, continued, "Souzan, you'll never guess who it is."

After the usual greetings of hugs and kisses between Emre and bewildered Yoran and Souzan, I was introduced as a friend of Emre, not a son-in-law.

Yoran anxiously asked, "Emre, is there any reason you should visit us after such a long time?"

Emre replied, "Could we sit and talk?"

Yoran, looking at Souzan, asked, "Talk about what?"

"I have some questions to ask, that's all," Emre said apologetically.

I could see the colour drain from both Yoran and Souzan's faces. Immediately, Souzan snuggled close to Yoran. He put his arm around her as though she was going to collapse. "Yes, come in, please do," Yoran said, trembling.

He led us into the lounge and asked us to sit. As we sat down, Yoran asked, "Is it the unwelcome news we have been waiting for? As a doctor, I have done what you two are doing so many times, so please get it over quickly."

Emre replied, holding one of their hands, "We have news of your daughter."

Both were shaking and crying. Souzan eventually said, "Inshallah, we have been waiting so long. Now we can grieve."

"No need for that. We think we have found Amina."

Yoran asked, "Are you sure it's Amina? Where did you find her?"

Emre indicated that I should answer the question by nodding at me. I replied, "We found her living in a Bedouin camp."

"She is alive and well?" they both cried out simultaneously.

"She has to be identified before we can be sure, but looking at Souzan, I don't think she could be anyone else."

"When can we see her?" Souzan pleaded. The expression on both faces now elated.

Yoran's shaky voice repeated, "When can we see her?"

"Sorry, not for a while. It's complicated."

"Please, there must be a way of seeing her now," Souzan retorted, tears streaming down her face.

"We have waited long enough; how are we supposed to cope knowing she is alive and well? Tell me that?" Yoran said fiercely, staring at me, waiting for my reply to confirm he was right.

So, I explained the situation thoroughly and advised them to employ a good lawyer. Emre added, "I can secure the services of a brilliant lawyer if you trust me."

When we said goodbye, they had calmed down a little. However, the excitement, anticipation, and trepidation were still evident on their faces. Emre agreed to be the go-between to relay information. We left an excited Yoran and Souzan planning their future. Any concerns that Amina returning to her parents would not be the best option had vanished. Any doubts I may have had that the Yassins were not Amina's parents evaporated. Amina bore no visible features of Yoran, a tiny man whose nose and ears seemed too large for his balding, grey-haired head and matching beard. But she was the spit of Souzan in every way. Later, I would learn the attributes of her father were more obvious yet invisible once I got to know her intellectually.

The weekend flew by, and I was back into the same boring routine of observing what was happening at the refinery. My friendship with Allan grew. I think that he enjoyed my company as much as I did his. I felt guilty that Allan didn't realise he was being spied on him through hidden CCTV. So, at one of our get-togethers, I planted a seed that I was aware and could see what was happening. He was slow on the uptake but eventually worked it out, causing a blazing row. At the time, I thought it could threaten our friendship. I strived to convince him that it was because I could see what he was forced to do – and his reactions to it – that I admired him. After much cajoling, Allan accepted what I was doing wasn't personal, and he could see the need.

Emre phoned from time to time to let me know what was happening with the Yassins and their lawyer. I was surprised the lawyer blocked them from visiting their daughter in prison. The case against the Bedouins was defended by a court-appointed lawyer, so the trial proceeded quickly.

Chapter 9
The Trial, 1996

The Bedouin trial outcome was as expected; two men and three women were found guilty. As predicted, the Bedouin's defence lawyer offered no mitigation other than they were destitute and had families to support. So, the anticipated life sentences were served as punishment. Yassin's lawyer managed to keep Amina in the dark regarding the whereabouts of her parents, and they were desperate to see her. After an extensive search, she was told they could not be located and was promised a more comprehensive search would occur if she was found innocent. The public-funded security police could not commit resources to a person likely to be found guilty of a crime. This did not sit well with Amina because, in her eyes, she believed she was innocent and worried she would be found guilty. She realised the lawyers' other argument was that it would be cruel for her parents to see her and then lose her again, making it more difficult for everyone. So, Amina reluctantly agreed not to discuss her parents and wait for the trial's outcome.

During the prosecution counsel's cross-examination of Allan, he tried to imply that Amina was complicit in the kidnapping by raising his voice vehemently and accusing Allan of lying about Amina's involvement. Allan stood firm and accused the prosecution of saying untrue things by answering the accusations with a firm, 'untrue' or 'no' response. Until then, Amina stood, head bowed in the dock, looking forlorn. When the prosecution pushed Allan to admit that their relationship was of a sexual nature, Amina's shoulders drooped even further. There was a slight delay between the translated questions and answers. Allan angrily denied the accusation, firmly, saying, "You are distorting the truth; she is not like the others; they're Bedouin, she is Syrian."

The lawyer snarled to the court's amusement, "How do you know that?"

Looking at the judges, Allan replied, "Because she told me so."

The lawyer laughed, then said, "And how did she tell you?"

While waiting for the interpreter's translation, Allan realised that the prosecutor knew his Arabic was poor but was unaware that Amina could speak some English. So, Allan retorted firmly, "She told me in English that she was Syrian, and her name was not Habiba, but Amina."

As soon as Allan had spoken these words, the courtroom started laughing until she raised her head in defiance and looked at them, pulling back her head covering. Immediately after she did this, a man and woman cried from the side gallery as they stood up, "Amina, eb-na, tee!"

Amina, with tears streaming down her face, cried back. "Baba, Mama!"

The laughter in the court stopped as they all realised simultaneously that Allan was telling the truth. Realising a lost child was reaching out to her parents, the spectators' silence was replaced by angry yelling. "Harij ealayk!" (Shame on you). This was directed at the prosecutor and the Bedouins in the dock. The courtroom was brought to silence by the head judge banging his gavel in an attempt to bring quiet to the court. The defence lawyer had planned that something like this would occur, thus alleviating long arguments and cross-examinations.

In English, the head judge looked at Amina and asked, "Child, what is your name?"

In English, she replied, "Amina Yassin, my father, Yoran, and my mother, Souzan, are there." She pointed at her joyful, crying parents.

The judge then addressed the crying couple, "Is this your child?"

"Yes," Yoran replied, his arms still extending, attempting futilely to touch Amina. Souzan nodded in agreement, with arms outstretched to get as close as possible to her child.

The court gallery was transfixed by the interaction and clapped as the swift verdict by the judge was announced. "Amina Yassin, you are found not guilty on all charges with immediate effect. You are released into the custody of your parents."

During my get-togethers with Allan, he always denied his feelings for Amina were obsessive. It was apparent that this was the case; maybe he was in denial, but it was evident to me. As he constantly manipulated our conversations to be about her, it reminded me of the conversations I had with George and the advice he gave me regarding Margaret. Allan was more experienced than me; he was once married and had fathered children. I thought he understood his feelings. I found this hard to understand until I discussed the issue with Margaret. Even though she had not met Allan yet, she built a picture in her mind from what I told her. She understood he was wary of letting his emotions get out of control in fear of being hurt again. Allan had put so much into his previous failed relationship that his self-esteem was shattered. So, regaining confidence and removing the doubt that something similar could happen again and him being worthy of a relationship was a work in progress.

Margaret also reminded me of a comparable situation when I met her; she'd called me 'an idiot abroad'.

I replied, "An idiot, maybe, only as far as you're concerned."

"Ali, he's just like you. He needs a push."

Emre and the Yassins reignited their old friendship. Often, they entertained each other in each other's homes. I would bump into them occasionally at Emre's, so I got to know Yoran better.

Emre told me that Yoran was very inquisitive about Allan regarding what sort of man he was. Emre already knew from me that I thought Allan was unconsciously fixated on Amina. So Emre told him everything he had learned about Allan was from me. Yoran didn't trust me yet to ask about Allan directly. Traditionally, trust must be earned and not given freely and should be mutual for a friendship to develop. After I allowed Emre to share with Yoran the videotapes of Allan at work, Yoran's confidence in me grew, and we became more friendly. However, the relationship between me and Emre was kept a secret.

On one of my visits to Damascus, Emre asked me to attend a social meeting with Yoran. Emre was impressed with the Yassin's house and garden and wanted to show me. It was a more traditional house than Emre's modern home. We spent our time there mainly outside in his beautiful natural garden, which impressed me. When Yoran greeted us, it was evident that I had gained his trust by the warmth and length of his embrace. I returned his hug with the same intensity; we were now friends. Souzan and Amina didn't join us in the garden, although Souzan brought refreshments. The difference in the manner of the Yassins since Amina had returned was evident; their worried faces had changed into open and smiling ones, at last at ease.

I didn't realise then that the casual meeting topic would eventually turn to Allan. *The reason for my invitation?* Yoran questioned me about my opinion of Allan. What sort of person was he? Did I trust him fully? Yoran asked if I thought Allan would agree to meet him at his home. I knew Allan would jump in with both feet for a chance to see Amina again, though the meeting was between Yoran and Allan. It was custom for unrelated sexes not to mix within households. Men and women had separate rooms for entertaining friends of the same sex. I told Yoran that Allan was due on leave soon and would be in Damascus and asked if he wanted me to tell Allan he would like to thank him. Yoran agreed that it would be nice if I could arrange it.

All I had to do was put the seed into Allan's head, which was simple, as I could tell he was up for it.

So, a meeting was arranged at Yoran's house. Allan assumed it would be just himself and Yoran because

I told him that. It was to begin with, Allan was aware that males and females had separate quarters in most Muslim households. When a male or female guest arrives, he is shown to the appropriate room. This is precisely what happened. During their conversation, Yoran asked Allan if it would be okay for his wife and daughter to join them. Allan was delighted and said as much. What happened next, Allan later told me, was bizarre.

Later, I asked Yoran what happened, and in his words, he said, "Souzan and Amina entered the room, sat in the corner, and had no part in the conversation. Allan couldn't take his eyes off Amina, but neither Souzan nor Amina looked in his direction."

I never told Allan that it was a set-up and that Yoran was judging Allan's reaction to Amina. At the same time, Souzan instructed Amina not to look at Allan; instead, she asked if she could sense that Allan was in the room. If so, what did she feel? Amina replied that she felt nervous and excited and found it hard not to look at him. "I can feel his eyes on me and wanted to acknowledge them."

Leaving Yoran's house was the only time Allan and Amina could make eye contact. Yoran and Souzan analysed their reactions, confirming their attraction to each other was mutual. Yoran invited Allan to attend a small garden party the following day. Allan, excited with the anticipation of seeing Amina again, accepted. So, the honey trap was set. Unknown to Allan, Margaret and I had input into the entrapment.

The day of the garden party was when Allan saw the real me. He had already received one shock – me spying on him at the beginning of our friendship. Spying on him was one thing, but not disclosing I was married was another problem; after all, we had become friends. Would he understand the fabricated reason why I kept it hidden from him? The real reason was to protect Emre, which always had to remain a secret. So, when I introduced Allan to Margaret as my wife, that was a shock. Margaret's open friendliness towards Allan diffused the situation when she told him how much she had been looking forward to meeting him.

Slowly but surely, the connection between Allan and Amina was clear for all to see. Margaret and I, encouraged by Yoran and Souzan, discreetly pushed Amina and Allan closer together. Margaret planned to take Amina on a shopping trip with Allan and me as escorts. That way, the interactions between the besotted couple would be without Amina's parents' scrutiny, removing their shyness towards each other.

Yoran decided to encourage the blossoming relationship by telling Allan and Amina he knew about their feelings for each other separately and encouraged them to seek each other's company openly. We all tried to make it easy for them to be together at every opportunity.

Eventually, it was plain to see how in love they were. Yoran confronted Allan on his intentions towards Amina. The idea of marriage was not in Allan's mind until Yoran put it there. Yoran brazenly approached Allan, offering the chance to propose marriage to Amina. Allan was shocked at the suggestion until Yoran told him Amina had agreed it was what she wanted. Yoran explained that most traditional marriages were arranged between the bride and groom's parents. But he didn't want his daughter to marry someone she didn't choose herself.

Amina had chosen him, and he thought she had made an excellent choice. Allan argued that they hardly knew each other, and Yoran knew little about him. Yoran implied he knew enough, but when questioned regarding the source of information, Yoran was reluctant to disclose it. Allan assumed it all came from Margaret and me and said so. Yoran did manage to convince the already lovestruck Allan to propose to Amina.

Unknown to Allan, Yoran was also discussing with Emre and me a new role for him at the university in the engineering department. Witnessing Allan's enthusiastic engagement with the Syrian national trainees on the videotapes impressed us all. I asked Allan if it would be something he would be interested in full-time. Allan was keen on the idea. His expression showed enthusiasm as he enjoyed working with young people who wanted to learn and better themselves. He was also unhappy in his current role, realising his situation was untenable unless there was a drastic change. Allan never knew how much Emre was responsible for his new position. He did assume it was partly down to me but earned mainly on merit. So when I told Allan that a job at the university had just come up and he should apply, Allan was delighted. The role was to establish a proper training regime for engineering students. Now, Allan would be a part of that change and looked forward to the challenge.

After Allan and Amina married, they moved into their first home together, an apartment supplied by the university. Allan and Amina's social circle was small, just her parents, Margaret, and me. Margaret and I became good friends with them, and we spent much time in each other's company. In fact for us, Allan, Amina, Yoran, Souzan, and Emre were our only real friends.

Margaret's influence on Amina brought about a change in her. She began to emanate some of Margaret's traits, becoming more outspoken and valuing herself as an equal to any man. She was intellectually superior to the rest of us in many ways, just like her father. Margaret encouraged Amina to enter further education as a student; she did exceptionally well and graduated with an English language degree. Our lives were intermingled with theirs, and I felt mutual respect.

Amina and Allan invited us to their place for a celebration meal when the overjoyed couple announced they would be parents. Margaret and I were thrilled for them, although we were both envious. But that all changed with the birth of their first child, a daughter they named Amara. Amara became the focus of our lives. It was the nearest Margaret would come to having a child. I, too, was drawn towards the baby girl; everything she did was unique to us. Every time we saw Amara, we were enthralled that she could now do this or that. Just over a year later, Amina and Allan had a second child, a boy they named Amal. He looked so different from Amara; with golden skin and blond hair, he was the opposite of the beautiful black-haired Amara. As they grew older, it was plain that Amara took after Amina in many ways. While Amal had the personality and mannerisms of Allan. Again, we both became enchanted by the new arrival, which we felt was part of us.

My life was perfect. Margaret was happy; she accepted that she would never have children. The James children were an ideal substitute for not having children of her own. As godparents to both of them, we treated Amara and Amal as though they were our own. Margaret often used the word 'lend' when asking to babysit, as though she was borrowing them for pleasure. Later, when they were older, she used the phrase 'borrow' to take them out for the day. The James family replaced the family I would never see again. I often wondered if my family would ever forgive me and if I would see them again.

Chapter 10

Civil Unrest

The government started to crack down on the unrest in Syria, making my role in the army more difficult. I was ordered to quell the peaceful protests by forcefully arresting and turning a blind eye to soldiers physically assaulting men, women and children, whose only crime was to attend meetings with others, hoping the government would listen to their voices. After all, it surely must be evident to the government things could not continue.

The peaceful protests achieved nothing; the people became frustrated and joined with more militant demonstrators, escalating anger by both sides. Being a soldier trained to follow orders without thinking of the consequences began eating away at my conscience. Maybe because of my time living in England, I saw how different things could be. As a liberal, I could see why there was unrest. I could see why there was discontent and how other things could be. Syria had become prosperous, but the wealth only reached a specific number of people. The working people creating the wealth could see this and wanted a little more; the government was unbowing. Demonstrations against the government erupted in most cities.

My role was to forcibly arrest the protestors and transport them to the courts to be punished. I was uneasy with that as I sympathised with the dissidents and found it challenging to comprehend why the government took such an uncompromising stance against its people. So, reluctantly, I retired from the army with Emre's help and influence. Emre found me a position at Al Farat Oil Company as a security advisor.

My role was similar to my previous one; monitoring activity and security. But now, as a civilian, my position would have more significant input. My role expanded to cover fraud and recruitment. Instead of following army orders, I was now a civilian in complete control. I oversaw a more interactive system to ensure the security of the refineries and the integrity of the plant and employees. The team under my supervision included accountants, auditors, ex-military police and fraud specialists. I would be part of the vetting process for all employees, including senior management, foreign nationals, and locals.

Then, the Syrian civil war erupted, and everything changed. The government brought the full might of its armed forces, with the help of its allies, and pummelled the cities where there was unrest. Instead of quelling the discontent, it induced militant Islamists throughout the Middle East to flood into Syria. The response from the government was to increase the bombardment of cities.

A national defence team was formed; their role was to help and rescue people caught up in the onslaught by saving them from the devasting attacks on civilian infrastructure. The defence team, known as the White Helmets, was led by a man called Raed al-Salah. It was an organisation of 2,500 men and 300 women who dedicated their lives to saving others. They rescued people regardless of ethnicity, religion, or politics. Their motto from the Quran is, 'Whoever saves one life, it is as if they have saved all of humanity'.

The government, now supported by Russia and various opposing factions, was indiscriminately attacking each other. The Syrian regime and Russia deliberately rained bombs, rockets, and improvised devices on the people to destroy the habitat of those caught up in the conflict. The casualties included soldiers, terrorists, men, women, and children. Both sides had difficulty recovering the dead and injured as they, too, were targets when they tried to do so.

I decided I could no longer stand by and watch. I couldn't take sides either. For me, the National Defence Forces was the solution, with no affiliation to any side. Though hundreds of White Helmet volunteers were killed, they did so while saving hundreds of thousands of lives. For every person's life they rescued, five more were killed. Though it was thwarted by unknown danger, I had to do something.

I begged Margaret to leave Syria and return to the UK. She wouldn't listen to me or her father, who also begged her to go, but she couldn't leave behind the only two people she loved. If her father and I were staying, she would too.

With factions indiscriminately swopping alliances, it was difficult to know what side they were on or what their objectives were. There were others like me in the same position, not precisely neutrals, as we all had some allegiances. We put them aside and helped those in need regardless of affiliation. They were all human beings and deserved to be saved, so a uniform or flag was inconsequential; they were all victims.

It was challenging, not knowing where and when the attacks would come from and in which direction. Whether drones, rockets, missiles, artillery or small arms combat weapons, the results would be the same: people were expendable. The government and allies targeted populated areas to break the people's will. Their lives were insignificant compared to the territory gained.

The level of devastation varied according to the tools of war used. The casualties changed, too. Some were buried, and others were burnt or had bullet or shrapnel wounds. Many were injured and soon would die. We tried to save as many as possible with our limited resources; those with a chance of survival were placed into ambulances, trucks, cars, or any mode of transport available. Unlocated buried bodies became apparent as the stench of rotting corpses filled the air.

Saving the living was the priority. The dead would have to wait. The doctors at the hospital treated each casualty in order of urgency. As opposing forces gained ground, the hospitals came under the authority of the occupying army. The occupying power did discriminate on who was treated. Those loyal to their cause took precedence over those desperate for treatment. Non-government hospitals were targets and bombed as the injured arrived to cause even more terror. This was a different type of war. There were no rules, no conventions, just bloody mayhem.

The Kurdish YPJ and YPG were hated by the government, ISIS, Al-Qaeda, Turkey, and other terrorist organisations. Sending Kurds in an ambulance to any hospital, not within Kurdish jurisdiction meant certain death. After one air raid, we attended the wounded in a bombed-out building, which a small group of YPG soldiers defended. Evidently, they had fought fiercely by the number of casualties and the state of the building peppered by light artillery. It resembled a slab of Emmental cheese – full of holes. We had to get the injured to a safe place before they were overrun. We treated the walking wounded during the lull in fighting – the lull possibly due to the restocking of artillery ammunition. How to get the severely injured to a hospital for treatment was a problem. If we took them to any hospital, not under the control of the Kurds, they would be sent to almost certain death. This put us in a difficult position.

The officer in charge of the Kurdish soldiers asked me to talk to his commander over the radio. The officer I spoke to was the YPJ commander, Rojda Felat. After a discussion, we decided to set up several secure rendezvous locations she would select according to the circumstances. She and only she would supply the coordinates so the wounded could be taken to a safe zone for handover. Rojda Felat gave me a password, allowing me to communicate with her. She insisted I give my real name as my password for security as I would be her only contact.

Handovers of injured Kurds became a regular occurrence. Over time, we saved many YPG and YPJ casualties, which must have frustrated all the other factions involved. Rojda Felat organised virtual free passage through most war zones to enable safe drop-offs.

The Syrian regime and its allies started a new tactic of fear. Instead of trying to gain ground by attacking the opposition, they levelled the ground by indiscriminately destroying buildings, schools, and hospitals. Anywhere that people sought shelter was targeted.

The National Defence team expanded and was joined by James Le Mesurier, an ex-captain in the British Army, financed by the British government. As the war intensified, it got increasingly hazardous, and the horrors of war increased. The white helmet clearly represented who you were and for what it stood. Whatever side we helped was grateful we were there for them but resented that we would treat their opposition equally. Some of the extreme radicals saw us as a threat, and we sometimes were targeted by them.

Understanding the ideology of each faction was difficult as most of them didn't know themselves. As leaders changed, their stances differed to suit the circumstances. Changing sides wasn't easy for those fighting in the conflict. The Free Syrian Army, Kurdish rebel fighters, Islamic State, Jabhat al-Sham, Hezbollah, and the Syrian Democratic Forces engaged in killing each other with varying success.

Some radical rebel fighters' doctrine was that anyone who didn't agree fully was opposed to them was the enemy. Therefore, they were infidels to be executed as they were against the will of their version of Allah.

The White Helmets also became targets even though they were not fighters but because they were saving the lives of their opposition. I didn't carry a gun, as to do so would most certainly lead to involvement in the war. Sometimes, I came under fire, and the only option was to hide. I felt like a coward, hiding from men untrained and undisciplined in soldiering.

Some rebel soldiers wore stolen white helmets removed from members of the defence team after they murdered them. As much as possible, our team kept to themselves; we knew and trusted each other. Sometimes, our team mixed with other White Helmets when the situation demanded it.

Occasionally, rebels wearing white helmets joined our little band. Still, I could tell by how they merged indifferently and were uncommitted when required; they were not one of us. It gave them an advantage as the opposition could wrongfully ignore them – to their peril. I had no alternative but to eliminate them as quietly and quickly as possible using the only tool of war I carried an army knife.

I never felt any remorse as I discarded their bodies. In the beginning, I killed them without anger; it had to be done for the safety of our group. Most of the defence team were shopkeepers, accountants, tailors, and market traders, not ex-soldiers like me. Though they were brave men and women, taking another's life was out of the question for them. Though they were grateful I was keeping them safe, they never thanked me for it. I understood why they closed their eyes to it. As the conflict dragged on, killing innocents became more brutal and commonplace. The evidence was displayed as a warning to others. Slowly, uncontrollable anger built up inside me. I ensured that the last person the perpetrators would see in this life was me when I killed them. I enjoyed the fear in their eyes as I cut their throat, whispering 'Ali Mansour' so they would be the last words they would hear in this life.

There was a lull in the bombing. *I'm exhausted; it's time to rest somewhere safe.* I entered a large storage building hardly damaged by the last raid, looking for a quiet corner, maybe some soft furnishings to lie upon. As I approached a likely area, a White Helmet I didn't recognise appeared out of the gloom, walking towards me. I could see he wasn't the stature of the rest of my team. Over two meters tall with broad shoulders, his jacket bulged, obviously hiding something. *Another one to kill, shit. I need a rest.*

He shouted, "Hey you!" I ignored him. "It's Ali, isn't it? Yes, it's you, Ali Mansour."

He must have been watching me. He spoke too quickly to recognise me instantly.

"Ali Mansour?"

At first, I didn't recognise him. Then, it all came flooding back when I saw the muscular Neanderthal forehead of my ex-unarmed combat trainer. *Sergeant Mostafa?* "Mostafa! What are you doing here?"

"You made captain, I hear?"

Think, think, make sure, and be careful. "Yes, what are you doing here?" *This evil bastard taunted and beat us cadets, demoralising us for pleasure.*

"What's with the White Helmet, Ali?

I asked him again, "What are you doing here?"

"Same as you, Ali."

"Sergeant, who are you with?"

The sergeant's stance changed; he braced his legs wide apart as his eyes scanned the area. "Ali, who are you with?"

I looked at his face; he was scrutinising me up and down. I knew from his training course what was about to come. I have never forgotten his words, which now resonate in my head. *Be the first to move; the element of surprise wins; commit fully; hold nothing back.*

I looked at him again. He stood like a second-row rugby forward, unstoppable. Then I remembered what young Alfie told me: 'The bigger they are, the harder they fall; hit them low and hard, make sure your head is on the right side, then pump your legs as hard and fast as possible'.

That was my element of surprise; with no weapon in my hands, I drove my body at his, hard and fast, low like a rugby prop, engaging with a second-row forward, pumping my legs on engagement. The sergeant was taller than me, so hitting him below his centre of gravity was easy. I crashed him against the wall behind him. *Young Alfie would have been proud.*

Metal objects concealed inside his jacket whacked against my collarbone on impact. He gasped for air; his empty lungs demanded oxygen.

The element of surprise is now gone; act quickly. I lifted him onto my shoulder and drove him to the floor, a perfect spear tackle worthy of a red card. I ensured that his head took the full impact of our combined weight. I heard a crack as his head hit the concrete floor, then a raging grunt as his massive hands locked onto my throat. I reached into his shirt and pulled out a combat knife; holding the pommel against my stomach, I arched my back and drove myself onto the sergeant with all my weight. Our stomachs touched as the knife plunged to the hilt below his rib cage. My stomach was warm and wet. I looked down at the screaming sergeant, remembering what he had trained me to do in this situation: *Finnish him off.*

I removed the knife from his stomach, grabbed his chin, and forced his head back to greet his begging eyes.

"I am Ali Mansour; you trained me well." I slit his throat, watching the terror in his eyes as the realisation of death flooded his face as he gurgled his last breath.

I was so tired of war. On my visits home to be with Margaret, I only wanted rest and sleep. The war had taken its toll on me. The happy, jovial, loving husband I wanted to be was emotionally drained: locked away in this nonsensical war. I could see that the war had affected Margaret, too. She made no funny quips anymore and looked drawn and tired; we were like androids going through the motions, not experiencing any pleasure. Margaret no longer sought the closeness of our bodies, nor did I, as we lay together at night. She seemed cold and distant. Something in her had changed. I had changed, too, as I didn't seek physical love either.

What is the matter with me? What's wrong with Margaret? So, I spoke, "Margaret, is there something wrong? Have I done anything to upset you?"

"No, Ali, you have done nothing wrong; it's just this bloody war."

"But you seem different towards me, not as loving." *Is there anyone else? What is wrong with me to think that?*

"I feel the same way as you. Something has changed in you too."

"You're right. This bloody war has changed us; I am not the same man. We have both seen too much suffering; I am sorry for that. Please forgive me."

"Ali, it's not your fault; I am a grown-up. I decided to stay with you. Nothing has changed; I don't want anyone else."

"You could have stayed with Emre. At least you would have been safe."

"That's too far away. I might never have seen you again. Imagine how I would feel then."

I hoped for rest and normality away from the conflict, but my mind was too full of horrors, some of which I had committed. I forced myself to focus on the good times. As hard as I tried, the nightmare of what I had seen and what I had done flooded my brain. *Am I becoming one of them? Do I enjoy killing? What will happen to Margaret? When will it end? What is the point of life?*

We didn't discuss the inhumanity we both witnessed every day. The poor people I rescued from their bombed homes. They were the same people Margaret and the doctors tried to save. So, we were both aware of the futility of this ridiculous waste of life and suffering.

I regretted not insisting that Margaret escape Aleppo with our friends, Allan and Amina. *Why did I let her insist she could stay?* The toll on her mental state and physical well-being showed. Before all this, she always dressed immaculately. Her hair and skin were without a blemish. Now, she didn't care what she looked like.

I often pleaded, "You should escape; it's not too late."

"Not without you," was always her reply.

So, I promised her, "My next call of duty is my last; we will go as there's nothing left to fight for."

"Promise me, Ali, one more week. I will wait for you."

The situation worsened as the bombing intensified. Chemical bombs were now dropped on innocent people, slowly torturing and killing the youngest with the most delicate lungs. If they did survive, their lives would be changed forever. *We can't cope. Too many casualties. We can do nothing.* There weren't enough face masks for everyone. I felt guilty wearing mine while others died, but without the White Helmets, nobody would survive.

Chapter 11
Raqqa Prison, 2014

Mohammed and his small band of rebels presumed I would be a valuable source of army intelligence. So, I was chained up in a truck along with other captured men, women, and children. Some were obviously captured Syrian Army soldiers, opposing rebel fighters, and others were ordinary citizens. All to be punished, perhaps for not agreeing with the ideology of their captors. Some were injured, confused, or dying. Most attempted to get themselves as comfortable as possible on the rigid steel deck, which jolted over the uneven road surface, making this impossible. The strongest forced others to squash together, using their feet as leverage. A few others, like me, strong enough to stand, held onto the side of the truck as best we could. The journey took about five hours over rough terrain in stifling heat. The stench of foul, stinking bodies and human waste induced stomach-wrenching nausea. At least while standing, the air was less putrid. The intentional lack of water or care ensured that some old, sick, or injured didn't make it. Only when the truck infrequently stopped could we discard the dead on the side of the road. So, on arrival at our destination, the truck was far less crowded.

My first interrogation started as a friendly affair, which didn't last long. Probably because Mohammed had bragged, I had vital information and would give it to them quickly to gain some kudos. I was offered a chair and sat opposite two interrogators across a small table. They provided fresh water and bread, which I devoured immediately. They treated me in a friendly manner, smiling like we were friends. One of them sarcastically enquired, "Was your journey pleasant?"

Things changed quickly when I didn't give them the correct answers to their questions. They assumed I was still a Syrian Army captain, as they had been led to believe by Mohammed, no doubt said as a feather in his cap. Their friendly attitude changed when I denied this.

Noticing their demeanour shift, I told them, "I am a White Helmet and saved many of your comrades from certain death."

The mention of White Helmets brought about a swift change in their attitude. I saw the rage in their eyes as they came closer.

They forced me to my feet and roughly manhandled me into a large, dimly lit room opposite. Agricultural and blacksmith tools, hammers, pliers, shears, tongs, and chains were hanging from one wall. On another were electrical cables and clamps, a small generator placed beneath. Two men dressed in rubber aprons sat at a table with various workshop tools scattered on it. They laughed as I was thrown onto the floor beside a dentist's chair. Dragged to my feet, a man on either side of me grabbed my arms, forcing me onto the chair.

One of the men standing beside me snarled, "What is your rank, name and number?"

"I have no rank or number. My name is Ali Mansour."

I didn't see his fist before it smashed into my face. As it hit, I heard, "Liar. Infidel." Then came the pain.

The other man appeared at my other side. Then, between them, they strapped me tightly to the chair, leather straps around my arms and legs and another across my chest so I could hardly breathe. Then, my wrists and ankles were bound tightly with rope. Lastly, a leather strap tightened around my forehead onto the headrest.

One man spoke, in a matter-of-fact manner, "You have a choice; admit who you are now, or my friend will smash your ugly face to a pulp." He looked at the other man as though he was about to enjoy himself and shrugged. "It's up to you."

"I am Ali Mansour."

I felt the impact again from a fist wearing a coarse leather welder's glove. My mouth filled with blood and broken teeth.

One of them asked again, "Who are you?"

I spluttered, "Ali Mansour." Blood and teeth splattered down my shirt. *If I admit that once I was a captain, the torture would be more severe, or maybe they would execute me now.*

I lost consciousness after several punches to my face; the headrest on the chair ensured none of the force was lost on impact. When I did come around on the hard floor of a cell, my hands were chained behind my back. I tried to discover what they had done to my face by using my tongue to search my mouth. I checked my nose by trying to breathe through it. I forced open my eyes in an attempt to see. Where there were once smooth teeth, now there were sharp, jagged objects, bits of splintered teeth, bone, and blood. I spat out the debris so as not to choke. I couldn't breathe through my nose; *was it plugged?* I couldn't tell if my eyes were open or closed as it was still dark. My face felt numb, a constant ringing noise in my ears. I licked my swollen lips and tasted blood and old leather. I moved my arms and legs as best I could, breathed in, and exhaled deeply to assess what else they might have done to my body. *So far, my head has been their only target; what next?*

I must have been unconscious, as I didn't hear anyone approach. I was woken by a sharp impact on my ribs, *a boot,* then another kick and a shout. "Get to your feet!" I tried to stand but lacked the strength to use my legs alone. My hands searched for something to hold. I struggled to my knees and heard laughter as I was shoved to the floor again. My arms were clasped tightly as they dragged me. I could see through the slits of my swollen eyes I was back in the blacksmith's workshop.

Strapping me into the chair again, one of them said, "He doesn't look so pretty now."

The other replied, "Let's find some fresh meat to tenderise."

His companion laughed. "It's my turn."

Chapter 12

UK, 2014

The Antalya doctors advised that they had done all they could. A better outcome would be achieved if I was treated by experts in a specialist facility. The White Helmets were funded by the UK government, so with the help of James Le Messurier's staff, Margaret contacted Frimley Hospital, the centre for PTSD treatment in the UK. I went along with everything I was told. I wasn't strong enough; I understood but didn't have the will to object. Concentration caused confusion, and decision-making caused severe headaches, so I avoided thinking; mostly, I slept.

Seeing Margaret's beaming smile and watery eyes, she struggled to contain her excitement. I realised before she spoke that she had some excellent news as she blurted, "You're going to the UK to be fixed. It's all arranged, don't argue." I didn't have the will to argue. Margaret asked, "Shall I contact Allan and Amina?"

"Please, not yet. I don't want them to see me like this."

"They are worried about us; they should know we are well."

"But I am not well and don't want them to see me."

"But they should know."

"Okay, tell them we're safe if you want, but don't mention anything else, promise?"

"Promise. I will tell them tonight. Is that okay?"

"Whatever."

We landed at Heathrow Airport; it was an easier journey for me than expected as we had assisted boarding on and off the plane. I sat in a window seat so I wasn't bothered by other passengers. A porter wheelchaired me into the arrival lounge. Margaret pushed our baggage trolley not too far away. Crowds of people rushed around me like in a nightmare, some almost bumping into me; *am I invisible?* I closed my eyes. I wanted to scream, *Stop! Don't you know what you are doing?*

We stopped moving, and my wary eyes opened; Allan stood before me. What is he doing here? I don't want him to see me like this. Amina wrapped her arms around Margaret, hugging her and crying. I tried to stand and eventually did. Allan hugged me a little too hard, then less as he realised how much I had changed. I tried to look pleased. I don't want this.

Then Amina looked at me and said, "What have they done to you?" I could see the regret in her eyes as she said, "Sorry."

I looked at Margaret to show that I wasn't expecting this; she nodded and silently mouthed, "Sorry."

We sat at a table. Amina brought coffee, and they sat talking excitedly, tears in their eyes. Not for me, I hope; pity is the last thing I need. Unable to hear anything but a mumble, I turned to watch expressionless people rushing around aimlessly. I sensed Allan looking at me, trying to get my attention. I wish he would stop. I need to be alone. I want to scream. Margaret noticed I was distressed, smiled knowingly, nodded, and mouthed, "Okay." She then phoned the courier to come. Please come quickly. Minutes later, Inshallah, he's here.

Margaret spoke to Allan and Amina. *Promising to keep in touch?* Amina and Allan stood beside me, patting my shoulders, and tried to get my attention. I looked up at them, smiling as best I could. *I wish they would just go.*

At last, they did; we watched and waved as they disappeared. As they turned a corner, I said, "Why? Margaret, why? I asked you not to."

She mouthed, "I needed to see them, for me."

After being strapped in the dentist's chair for my second interrogation in Raqqa prison, I couldn't remember anything. *Why?* As much as I tried, it was a complete blank. Months had passed with part of my memory wiped; I couldn't remember what had been done to me. I knew the human brain could shut down memories that were hard to deal with after experiencing traumatic events. I witnessed other confused casualties of war, as it was commonplace. Soldiers were often disorientated and confused. Their memories were blocked for prolonged periods, sometimes never returning, depending on the individual's response to warfare or the extent of the trauma they experienced. They dealt with their anguish in isolation; I was one of them now. I wasn't aware of the full extent of the damage they did or how it was inflicted. I realised that my rehabilitation would take time. Not knowing how long it would be before my memory would return and how I would cope if it did or didn't, distressed me. I was determined to get physically well again, so my mind was occupied with ways of doing that, leaving little time to concentrate on anything else.

I could now stand unsupported for a little while and sit in a chair, exercising my arms and legs. I could see the damage done to my body and feel the weakness. Whenever I saw my reflection, it felt strange as it wasn't me I saw, so I avoided looking at the imposter pretending to be me. The hearing aids fitted in Antalya abruptly ceased working. I was back on headphones again but still found understanding speech difficult.

After the preliminary examination, I was taken to a private bedroom and shown how the nurse call and emergency system work. Within minutes of settling into my surroundings, a nurse entered my room with a plastic jug, cups, and a small container of pills.

Her name tag, Sheila, was pinned next to her upside-down watch. She insisted, "Take your medication immediately."

Sheila watched me swallow the assortment of pills before she left. At last, in peace and quiet, I could rest; I was so tired.

Did the nurse give me something to induce sleep?

I am awoken by a different nurse; it's morning. Confused that it was yesterday afternoon, I fell asleep. I feel different. People move slower now, not rushing anymore; my panic over their speed has been reset. After breakfast, a nurse pushes me in a wheelchair to one room after another for more tests. The same after lunch; more pills, tests, and later in my room, Margaret visits. *She has changed; she doesn't look the same as I last saw her.*

She mouths, "You look better."

I say back, "So do you." *Is it me that's changed?*

The following morning, more pills, a similar routine, room to room, different doctors, and further tests. This routine continues, sometimes seeing a doctor or nurse, sometimes a medication change, rest, and sleep for about a week.

Two doctors entered my room; Margaret was there, too. After they left, Margaret explained what they told her as best as possible by mouthing and pointing to the important bits from the leaflets they left us to read.

I learned they were conducting tests to discover the extent of my issues and planning an ongoing treatment schedule. The first thing they needed to sort out was my hearing, which would make communication easier. Not knowing what was going on was exasperating as I always needed to be in control of my situation and make my own decisions rather than having them made by someone who thought he knew what I was thinking.

Margaret mouthed, "An auditory brainstem implant is your best option." I nodded, and she added, "It will make a big difference."

The movements Margaret used to communicate with me unsettled me; she moved her head sharply, with her eyes wide open, showing alarm. My army training taught me to use my senses before I moved. So, I was agitated when things moved without sound, especially when they came into view without warning from behind.

The implant operation was successful. I could now hear most things except for high-register noise. Some sounds were annoying after being without hearing for so long; I forgot what a distraction hearing everything could be. But I slowly got used to being disturbed by things clattering around me.

The appointments with the medical team ceased for about a week or so to allow me to acclimatise to being able to hear. Margaret was allowed extra visiting time. Slowly, we were trying to piece together what had happened to me during the lengthy periods of lost memory. I realised I was selfish, and the conversation was always about me. I could tell Margaret had issues; something had changed her, but she replied when I tried to discuss it, "Not now, maybe when you're better." When I pressed her further, she shook her head, saying, "I remember everything vividly. I won't talk about it. I need to forget. It's this bloody war; you don't need to know."

"Margaret, I need to remember who did this to me and why."

"The answer is simple, Ali; psychopaths and sadists did it to you. They don't need a reason; they do it for pleasure."

So, I never pressed Margaret again on how bad it was for her. She only got annoyed when I asked. *Perhaps she needs to forget; strangely, I want to remember.*

The daily physio sessions helped with my movement. I slowly gained strength and a little weight. I was able to walk a little, but the effort was exhausting.

I was eating solid food, though the condition of my mouth didn't make it easy. The dentist insisted I wait until I was stronger so he could repair the extensive damage under anaesthetics.

The psychiatrist introduced himself as Mr. Keller. I thought he sounded German, but later I found out that he was, in fact, Swiss. He was abrupt, precise, authoritarian, and exuded confidence in his ability. So, I was assured I was in good hands.

He explained that he recently began using the Qigong technique to help with PTSD. It was a new procedure; he had reliable results, and all the feedback from others was that it worked well. I was apprehensive about whether moving my body into various positions would improve my cognisance. Mr. Keller insisted that Qigong exercises optimised energy within the body and mind. It had psychological and physical components, regulating thoughts, breathing, movement, and posture. But slowly, I was surprised the benefits began to show, and I became more relaxed.

Part 2
Margaret's Story

Chapter 13

1994

I first spotted Ali at a pub quiz. He seemed out of place, shy and nervous, so I was puzzled why he would be in the company of the well-known letch, George Newall. I wasn't puzzled why Kirstie wanted to join them at their table, as George was the sort of guy she was attracted to. Ali was quiet, unlike George. I noted by the colour of his skin, dark hair, and brown eyes that he was probably from the Middle East. The contrast between George and Ali couldn't have been starker. George was confident; he spoke loudly and assumed everyone would be interested in his inane banter. He was tall and thin with a spotty porcelain-white face and scraggy blonde hair. His unkempt look appeared to me to take time to perfect. *Done for effect, some girls like that; why?*

Ali was as tall as George, with broader shoulders and smartly dressed. He was too handsome for his own good. When we made eye contact, his deep brown iris contrasted sharply with the whites of his eyes. His skin colour enhanced his perfect white teeth when he smiled. A smile he would perfect when he became more confident in proving a point he was trying to make, and always used when greeting close friends and me. Although

Ali seemed shy when he went to the bar, he strode like an athlete. George shuffled as though everything was an effort. *What do these two have in common?*

It was obvious that George and Kirstie were hitting it off as the innuendos flew between them. It seemed to be going over Ali's head; he didn't appear to be listening or enjoying himself. I watched him sip his glass of wine as though it was the first time. *Maybe he is a Muslim? That figures. Does he know what the other two are planning? What would he make of that?*

A few weeks later, one of my fellow female student's swimming friends mentioned a gorgeous bloke she bumped into at the swimming pool at the beginner's session. From her description, it could have only been Ali. So I deliberately arrived early for my next swimming session and watched the learners from the gallery, hoping to glimpse the handsome man. There was no mistaking Ali; his swimming style was awful, thrashing the water instead of using it. He undoubtedly used a lot of energy, top marks for effort but nothing for technique.

On the spur of the moment, I joined the proficient session a little early as an opportunity to hopefully see him. I decided to bump into him accidentally on purpose by entering the swimming pool early, hopefully as he was leaving. He didn't notice me as I walked past him until I called his name, then pointed at myself and said, "Margaret."

Shyly but politely, he greeted me before walking away. His physique was more like an accomplished athlete than I had imagined. I was disappointed we didn't engage further. I started my regular swimming routine, length after length, until I was exhausted. As I rolled my head to one side to breathe, I spotted someone watching me from the back of the gallery. So, I pulled myself out of the water and glanced at the figure through my raised arms, in the diving position, for a better look. It was Ali. *Interesting.* I stood on the poolside and went through my diving routine as though I wasn't aware of him. Then, I continued my usual training routine, hoping my watcher would be impressed.

I went to the next training session earlier to watch Ali from the front of the gallery again. This time, I hoped he would notice me. He did, so I waved at him, using hand signals to indicate 'meet me for a coffee'. He looked surprised and confused but agreed to meet in the pool café.

Through my Arabic studies, I realised that Ali's shyness probably wasn't due to a lack of confidence. However, meeting an unchaperoned female would be a new experience, so I expected him to be unsure. *Meeting a non-Muslim woman? It would increase his trepidation.* I hoped he found me as attractive as I did him. I didn't understand my motives other than that he was handsome, and I was drawn to him. *Am I following in my mother's footsteps?*

I did convince Ali there could be a mutual advantage as I was studying Middle Eastern culture, so I could help with his written English. He could help me with my Arabic. *But is this my real reason?*

We often met, always away from inquisitive eyes. The more we met, my urge to get closer increased. I sensed that Ali had similar feelings. I thought Ali would never make the first move, but I was wrong. Ali made a subtle move by gently touching my back as he guided me through a doorway; it felt electrifying. I turned, faced him, and smiled; his apprehension disappeared into a lovely smile as we made eye contact. At that moment, everything changed. *Does he feel the same way?* I thought it was my responsibility to make my feelings absolutely clear. I knew what I wanted. Somehow, it had to be Ali's decision. *How do I persuade him to admit he feels the same as me?*

The opportunity arose as we did our usual stroll along the banks of the Isis. Ali's hand accidentally brushed mine. I made my move, and we soon held hands. I asked Ali if he felt the same about me as I did him. If he did, we should decide to stop seeing each other or let things take their natural course. Ali answered immediately that he wanted to keep seeing me. So I asked him to take time for his decision. He didn't take time, and that day, we became lovers.

After several days of discovering each other, Ali left my flat, planning to return later that day. Once alone, I realised that I hadn't been honest with Ali and told the whole truth about myself. I knew my feelings for Ali would grow and be challenging to break as time passed. Though I didn't want it to stop, it had to. It couldn't go anywhere. I was fooling myself, so I phoned Ali and told him it was all over. He wouldn't accept what I told him and became incredibly angry. He turned up at my flat and forced his way in, demanding an explanation. Eventually, I broke down and told him we were fooling ourselves. There was no way I could physically force Ali out of the flat. I sat on the bed, not looking at him, not saying anything until he explained that he had taken advice from George. *Bloody George, of all people.*

That made me truly angry; I screamed, "George is a womanising letch; what would he know about commitment?"

"Maybe nothing, but he is living for today."

"Ali, be sensible; I can't do that. It's hard now. It will be unbearable for me in a couple of years, or doesn't that matter to you?"

"Yes, it does matter, but that's in the future, not today, right?"

"You must return to Syria; you will want children one day. Ali, did it ever cross your mind I could become pregnant?"

"No, it wasn't in my mind."

"Well, it should have; what were you thinking?"

"Nothing."

"Exactly, Ali, it was lust. You men are all the same; you're just like George." *And my father.*

"Margaret, how can you say such things? I love and want to be with you; what I felt wasn't lust."

"Ali, just go, go now, please."

"I am not going anywhere until I convince you it isn't lust."

"You're just like my father. Once you go back, you won't return, will you?"

"Margaret, we will work something out in the future; let's live for today."

"There are things I kept from you of which I am ashamed. I should have been more honest. We wouldn't be having this conversation if I had told you in the beginning. Sorry, I didn't, so please just go now. It's over."

"Not until you tell me the real reason. I am not budging."

Why is he making it so testing? My father left my mother without regret. Why can't he? "If I tell you, promise me you will leave?"

"Promise."

I took a deep breath and told Ali the whole truth. About my cancer, how I was barren. I thought my father was an Arab who duped my mother and left her to raise his child alone. Ali sat and listened. There was no sign of disgust as he heard the truth. Secrets were out. Ali was the only person I bore my soul to. He just sat there with tears filling his eyes.

Ali didn't leave that night. First, we sat on the bed, not talking, and later, he lay beside me till the morning. *Ali is still here after I tried to drive him away; maybe he is different and accepts me for what I am, so perhaps George is right. Live for today. Listening to George, of all people.*

We made a pact that we could walk away at any time and live for today. We accepted that it wasn't forever, and our love grew stronger.

I felt Ali was not cut out for the army as our relationship grew. He was a kind, considerate man who always put others first. I never openly questioned him about how compatible his meekness was with being an officer in the army. But it did concern me that he wasn't suitable for that position, so I discreetly broached my concerns. Ali didn't understand why I was worried, so I explained that most men I had encountered tended to be aggressive. I used the word 'macho', which he didn't understand. So, I asked, "Why do you always give way in crowded places?"

His puzzled reply was, "It's polite to do so."

Because of Ali's physical stature, macho men often placed themselves in confrontational positions around him. Ali would smile and give way to them. It unnerved me, so I asked him why, and he replied, 'I have nothing to prove.'

"But they think they won and made you back down, right?"

'It doesn't matter what they think."

Ali's timidness disappeared one sunny morning when we were strolling along a winding path through a park, hand in hand, admiring the spring flowers starting to bloom. I felt my handbag ripped from my shoulder. Shocked, I screamed obscenities as the hooded perpetrator cycled along the path at speed, my bag slung over his shoulder, raising his front wheel off the ground. *A victory salute?*

I turned to Ali for help, but he wasn't beside me. He was running at a tangent to the thief. *Why isn't he chasing him? Bloody hell, Ali, man up.* Ali was running at speed but not upright; his body shape looked like a sprinter as it left the blocks, as though he was trying not to be seen; he weaved in and out of flower beds. Then, I noticed that the exit gate to the park was roughly in the direction he was running. Ali veered to avoid the gate and ran towards the park's boundary iron railings and hedge. He leapt in the air and grabbed a railing post, clearing the railing spikes and hedges and disappearing out of view. The thief cycled up to the gate and rode through.

The next thing I saw was the thief's bike sprawled on the pavement on the other side of the gate. I ran towards the exit gate to see Ali holding the thief by his left shoulder and right arm. The hooded thief appeared frozen, crouching like he was expecting to be beaten. Ali released the thief's right arm, placed his fingers outstretched and pushed them into his stomach. The thief dropped to his knees, gasping for air. Ali pulled the thief's hood back to expose his face. I was expecting to see a youth. Instead, it was a man, possibly in his thirties. Ali removed a rucksack from the thief's back, then his hooded coat. Then, he emptied the contents of both onto the pavement. An array of stolen wallets, handbags, purses, phones, and bank cards fell onto the pavement. Ali then searched the coat and rucksack and found a knife in each and small packets of white powder.

Ali noticed I was watching and gave me my bag, saying, "Make sure nothing is missing." Looking at the thief, Ali said, "In my country, the punishment is simple. We cut off the right hands of thieves." Ali grabbed the man's chin and forced his head back, exposing his throat; holding a knife in his hand, he forced the thief to look at it. I could see the fear in the man's eyes. Ali then grabbed the man's right hand, moving it horizontally and mimicked cutting it off. He uttered, "It's a shame we are not in my country."

Ali glared at him, placed the knife blade where the metal gate was hinged and snapped the blades from both knife handles. Ali forced the man again to look at him, asking, "What do you want me to do with you?"

The thief replied, "Let me go. Promise I won't do anything like this again."

"You mean I should take the word of a thief? Do you think I am stupid?"

"Honest, I won't do it again."

"You're a professional making a living from stealing. Do you know how much pain and suffering you cause others?" The man remained silent, and Ali addressed me. "We have a couple of options: take him to the police or make him give back all he has stolen to the people he has mugged."

The thief butted in, in an Eastern European accent, "I give everything back."

Ali replied, "I thought you would say that."

I asked, "How are you gonna do that? You've spent a lifetime stealing."

A small gathering of passersby was watching what was happening by this time. Someone must have phoned the police; a police siren got louder as it approached. Two coppers jumped out of a police van, one large male and one female. I presumed that they interpreted that a fight was taking place. The male police officer grabbed hold of Ali. I assumed he thought Ali was the instigator and tried to lock him in a restraining hold. Ali manoeuvred himself from the grasp with ease and held the male police officer pressed against the railings, with both arms locked up his back. The female had her truncheon drawn and was about to use it when I and those observing the melee shouted, "You've got the wrong man!"

The thief took his opportunity to make a run for it; Ali must have seen it out of the corner of his eye. He released his hold on the male police officer, turned and removed the truncheon from the confused female police officer and threw it on the pavement. Within a flash, he had the thief restrained against the fence. Ali agitatedly told the embarrassed male police officer, "I think this is the one you want."

The group watching clapped and shouted sarcastically, "Well done!"

The two coppers sheepishly arrested the thief and locked him in the back of the van.

I witnessed my Ali – 'Mr Nice Guy' – turn into an 'action man' doing what he was trained to do. I was impressed by how quickly he weighed the situation and took immediate action. I knew he was a powerful athlete, but seeing him in action, I realised how fast and strong he was. My fears that he wasn't up to being an officer in the army were quelled immediately. I realised he meant it when he said he had nothing to prove. I watched more closely how he avoided confrontation with men. Though he often gave way, his manner showed he was giving way on his terms, and the other men knew. I always felt completely safe when out, wherever we were.

Chapter 14

The Destruction of Aleppo, 2013

We never saw much of each other as Ali's duties with the Syria Civil Defence unit meant he was away for prolonged periods. As the bombing of Aleppo increased, I saw him less. When the fighting began, it was between the government forces and factions trying to depose it. The government's aim was no longer to deplete the opposition in combat. Instead, they indiscriminately bombed Aleppo, raising it to the ground so nothing could survive or be worth fighting for. Those who could escape had left the city; those unable to go – or the belligerent – stayed and joined the rebels. Some fundamentalist rebels saw everyone as their enemy, even those fighting against Assad. Those who disagreed with the rebels' doctrine were executed brutally as an example to others. That put Ali and me in peril because he was a White Helmet, and I was neither an Arab nor a Muslim. The White Helmets were well-organised and prominent, less likely to be mistaken as opposition fighters. Still, some didn't agree with their principles, which put them at risk.

We had agreed to stay in Aleppo and help where we could, not realising that this bloody conflict would continue till there was nothing worth saving. My father insisted that I leave Aleppo and live with him in the safe part of Damascus under the control of the government. That would mean I would never see Ali, as the journey between Aleppo and Damascus was fraught with danger. My father was no longer a loyal government member but was afraid to speak out, as doing so meant execution as a traitor. He planned to escape and seek asylum in the UK and assured me the process was easy through his UK government contacts. He begged me to join him and convince Ali to join us.

When Ali did come home for a brief respite, I could see a deterioration in him. Constantly tired and irritable, he apologised when he realised his behaviour affected me. His appearance changed due to days without sleep and nourishment. Thinner and gaunter, his face showed the anguish of witnessing neverending death. He couldn't try to hide the effect with make-up like me.

He always planned that his visits would be more extended, but the sounds of the obliteration of Aleppo didn't permit it. His conscience stopped him from resting while others were helping those in a worse position than him. The only help the battered people got was from the White Helmets.

I hid from Ali what it was like for me; I knew he was doing the same thing. We didn't need to be reminded of the death of the blameless and the futility of it all. We tried to forget it, so I didn't talk about the war, and neither did he. I knew I was seeing the best of it: people who had a chance of survival that had been pulled from the ruins of their homes. Helping survivors, though sometimes only one survivor from a family would make it.

Dealing with their realisation in recovery was challenging when a father, mother or child realised they were now alone in their pain and grief. Not understanding the reason, we could never answer their questions. I became immune to despair, not that I didn't care, but because there wasn't time to console the grieving and, at the same time, help those struggling to stay alive. There were just too many of them.

Initially, I removed blood-soiled clothes, dust, and debris from their bodies so a doctor or nurse could spend more time attending to injuries. Then, clean the beds and bedding of those that didn't survive, ready for the next survivor. I would launder the clothes of those who no longer require them so those in need would have something to wear. When washed clean, clothes unfit for wear could be used as rags and dressings. I administered clean water and held their hands if I had time.

Most of the injured were in shock, and comforting them was little help. Those who could sit sat with glazed eyes, staring at nothing. Those who couldn't sit lay on beds or the floor, staring at the ceiling. The children were sullen, confused and asked, "Where is Mama or Baba?" I used to comfort the children and tell them everything would be all right. I soon realised getting attached emotionally made it worse for them and me. There wasn't time for that, as we had more patients and fewer doctors.

So, cleaning the wounds of the injured became more critical than cleaning beds. I was told what to use and how to use it. If the patient was conscious, washing away the filth from a large open wound without anaesthetic was physically and mentally demanding for me. The wounded lined the corridors, all demanding treatment.

Some were nursing their dead children or those with little chance of surviving.

I was so tired and emotionally drained. I couldn't do this anymore. *How can I tell Ali?* He needed rest and comfort, not me moaning about how difficult it was for me.

Often, I had to run the gauntlet as I walked through conflict areas, where groups of fighters gathered in dark corners. I frequently changed my route, wore a burqa, stayed in the shadows, and avoided anything that moved. It worked until one morning when I was in a hurry because I was late due to a bombing. Perhaps the rebel fighters noticed I was young because of my walking pace. From shadows, they jumped out, one in front of me and one behind, and dragged me back into the shadows. A hand covered my mouth while his other groped my breasts. I struggled as the other one smashed his fist into my stomach. Winded, I couldn't breathe. I gasped for air as my burqa was lifted to cover my face. They dragged me to the ground as fingers forced my burqa into my mouth. Then, one of them entered me; it was over in seconds. The one groping my breasts stopped, and then he entered me. I tried to fight, but it was useless; the more I struggled, the harder they hit me. How many times did this happen? I can't remember. My body was numb, and I felt nothing. They kicked me several times, calling me a whore as they left, laughing. The burqa saved my life; my fate would have been worse if they knew I was not Arab.

The rape only lasted minutes, but the effects would last a lifetime. *I feel ashamed. My fault? Dirty.* I was desperate to wash my body clean, wash away what had happened to me. When I reached the hospital, I entered the room where I cleaned the beds and stripped naked. Using a hosepipe and scrubbing brushes and disinfectant, I scrubbed myself until I bled. I washed the inside of me using a squeezy soap bottle to remove the revolting evil planted inside me. A female doctor entered the room and, realising what had happened, removed the bottle from me and gently washed my back and legs. She gently touched the black bruised places and asked if it hurt as she felt for broken ribs. At the same time, she asked, "Do you need to talk?"

I shook my head.

"Okay, later then, you need to talk. You will need cream to use below. Get dressed and come to my office for treatment."

"What with? You have no medicines left."

"I have saved some. Come when you are dressed, and I will give you an injection. You never know what diseases these dirty bastards are carrying."

I felt filthy because their sperm was inside. My anguish reached another level when I realised I could be infected by a dirty disease.

The doctor handed me clean rags and said, "Quickly dry yourself and come."

When the doctor left the room, I wretched at the impact of what she said. Uncontrollably acidic bile spurted onto the cleaning room floor. After drying myself, I dressed in the previously laundered clothes I had taken from the dead.

After the antibiotic injection, the doctor asked, "Do you need a contraceptive pill?"

"No, there's no need, thank God."

Fertile women who would carry the extra anguish of a child growing inside them. How could they bear evil growing inside their wombs? How could such a mother come to love her child conceived in this way?

The doctor came close, gently held my shoulders, looked into my eyes, and said, "Go home. You are done here."

"But I'm needed."

"It will happen again, and if they find out you are English, what they will do to you will be far worse."

"Worse, what could be worse?"

"An ambulance will take you home. You are finished here."

"But I can still help."

"Not if you're dead; please go."

I relive the nightmare of what happened that day; it's with me forever. For many nights, I had nightmares and relived the horror. It always ended the same; Ali came to my rescue, brutally beating the rapists. He then turned into one of them, enjoying the pain he was inflicting, evil in his eyes. When awake, I interpreted the nightmare; I feared what Ali witnessed would turn him into one of them.

The only respite Ali and I had was with each other. The war ensured these times were getting fewer, and we had little rest. 'Living for today' now had a different meaning. When we used the word 'living' before, it meant living life to the full. Living now meant surviving. We both knew it was only a matter of time before our luck ran out. Most of our neighbours and friends had either escaped or been killed. Those who remained hadn't the will to leave or fight; most were waiting for death as they had nothing to live for. Most of these people were elderly and had witnessed their children, grandchildren or partners killed, so they had nothing to live for. When we told them they must leave this place, they replied, "Where would we go?" Or they claimed their family was here, even though they were alone. They couldn't leave their dead behind because all they had were memories.

We had made a pact to leave Aleppo before it was too late. That day was upon us when Ali left me that morning, promising it would be the last time. It was a guilty relief that Ali caved in because of me. I didn't care. I couldn't witness death anymore. Imagining life without Ali was unbearable. So that morning, when he left, I prayed that Ali would soon return with a plan for us to get away safely.

I returned to my hospital duties, and, like Ali, I had to do something. The journey to the hospital was getting increasingly dangerous, so I stayed there and took a rest whenever I could. After a week, exhausted, I returned home and waited for Ali to return as promised. Ali usually phoned whenever he could, but sometimes it was difficult. So I wasn't worried more than usual that he didn't contact me. I waited, but Ali didn't come. The days drifted into weeks. *Where is he? Is he alive?*

Ali would never know what had happened to me. I couldn't compare the brutality he witnessed daily with my rape. Since that day, I carried a large meat knife tucked inside my burqa. I planned what part of the body I would chop off, so they couldn't gratify themselves again. *How can men behave like this? How have their minds become so twisted and evil? Do they have wives, families, and children? How can they love them and do this to others?*

Then, it became too dangerous to return to the hospital – what was left of it. Frequently, men gathered us together to witness their atrocities with glee on their faces. Euphoric, they conducted Allah's wishes, believing they would be rewarded in the afterlife. They forced us to watch them cut the throats of those who disagreed, removing their heads as a prize for their god. Sometimes, dozens of devout citizens who disagreed with their ideology were mass executed. Heads mounted on railing spikes, left to rot and decay in the sun as a reminder that it could be yours.

Sometimes, the crime was smoking, listening to music, singing, or showing affection to another male or female; any excuse to feed their psychopathic minds. Did these men praying to Allah five times daily justify their actions? It wasn't written in the Quran. No, the words came from the twisted ideology of the leaders that groomed them.

Assad's allies intensified the bombardment, and hospitals were now a legitimate target. Our apartment was still mainly undamaged, but all around me was destruction. Ali had never been away this long. *Something happened to him?*

My phone rang. It could only be Ali or my father. I picked it up before the third ring. I was shaking, and the line was quiet. "Ali, is that you? Daddy, are you there…?"

"Ali Mansour's wife, yes?"

"Yes… Why?"

"Ali is safe."

"Where is he?"

"You come now."

"Who are you?"

"White Helmets."

Is this a trick? Can I trust him?

"Rojda Felat, Ali's friend, asked me to collect you. You come now, yes?"

So, where's Ali? "Why can't I speak to him?"

"Not here."

"Where is he? Please, tell me."

"He's in hospital. Come now, please."

"Where to?"

"I will be outside; wait for me, okay?"

"Is he hurt?"

"Come now. We'll talk later, okay?"

"Who are you?"

"Friend of Ali, please come now."

Still unsure if it was a trap, I took the risk, packed a few things, and waited outside in the shadows of the façade. I expected whoever was picking me up to be waiting. I felt highly nervous without the burqa, vulnerable without its protection. Several vehicles passed by, but none stopped. *Have I been conned? Something isn't right.*

A car pulled up as I was about to give up and return inside. A man shouted, "Come quickly!" He waved his arms as though agitated.

I didn't move to begin with. *Something's not right.*

The man shouted again, "Hurry, please, we must go now!"

Reluctantly, I got in the car. *Was this man risking his life for me, or was he threatening mine?*

The driver said, "Me, Ahmed, you, please."

"Why did you take so long? I thought you would never come."

"Sorry, I had to change my route; bad men could stop me, understand?"

"Where are you taking me? How long will it take? Is Ali there?"

"Okay. Jindires, maybe one hour. Inshallah, Ali is in hospital."

"Where is he? Is he badly hurt?"

"Antalya, Türkiye, hurt, yes, I don't know how bad."

"Thank you, Ahmed. Sorry, I doubted you; you're risking your life for me, and all I do is question you."

"Mafi mushkila. Ali told me what you have been doing for my people." He pointed to a white helmet on the back seat.

"No problem, because Ali is your friend, yes?"

"Inshallah, he good man."

The point of my knife tucked in my waistband was digging into my thigh. I wriggled on my seat, put my hand on the handle and tried discreetly to adjust its position.

Ahmed noticed my fidgeting and demanded, "What are you doing?"

"Nothing, getting comfortable, that's all."

"No, you are hiding something; what is it?"

"Nothing."

"Liar, you must tell me if you have a weapon, yes?"

"Yes, a knife."

"Just like Ali."

"What do you mean?"

"Never mind. Has Ali taught you how to use it?"

"For God's sake, it's a knife; it's got a point on one end and a handle on the other."

"Please don't use that language. Has Ali taught you how to kill?"

"No need, I know what to do."

Ahmed stopped the car, angrily shouting, "Woman, the knife now!" He held out his outstretched hand. "Or we go nowhere, okay?"

"But it's for my protection."

"It will be your death; please give me the knife now."

"Death is a better option."

"I understand. I am here to protect you; now give me the knife, or we turn back."

Reluctantly, I handed him the knife; he ran his fingers over the blade. "Very sharp, good." Then, he placed it in the driver's side door panel compartment.

"Okay, now we go; please, no more surprises." As he revved up, he said again, "I keep you safe."

"You said that Ali carried a knife. How do you know? I have never seen it."

"Never mind, he is not here. That's not important."

The scale of destruction seemed more significant here than in Aleppo, as every building was destroyed as far as the eye could see. The odd wall, riddled with bullet or shell holes, stood out as a reminder that once it was inhabited. Burnt-out vehicles littered the road, evidence that those trying to escape the carnage were targeted. The black ISIS flag was raised in the centre of almost every settlement, confirming they were the victors and the prize they had won – which was worth little before destruction and nothing now. The stench of the dead was in the air. Humans and animals were left to rot; their stomachs swelled to bursting in the hot sun.

When we came to parts of the highway where Ahmed was unsure, he firmly pressed my head forward so I couldn't be seen. "Mushkilat kabira, woman," he uttered sharply every time he sensed danger. I ducked as low as possible to avoid being seen. Ahmed would say softly, 'Okay', to show the threat had passed. When we passed vehicles with smoke wafting from a recent attack, Ahmed stepped on the accelerator and patted my hand as we drove past them.

I ducked down as Ahmed uttered sharply, "Ayreh feek, the bastards, get down." He slowly braked. I heard the bursts of two automatic rifles rapidly firing into the air. Ahmed waved his left hand in a friendly gesture as we slowly came to a stop, smiling as if greeting friends. He wound his window down as though he was going to talk. I was hiding as low as possible. I saw the scowling face of a young, bearded man at the window. He indicated by waving his gun that Ahmed should get out of the car. Ahmed reached down – I thought for the door handle. I hid my face and then heard a thump. Startled, I looked up and saw the young man with an expression of disbelief as blood spurted onto Ahmed from a gaping wound in his neck caused by the knife Ahmed had taken from me. The car charged forward, hitting something heavy, making a soft thud. As we bumped over it, screams came from underneath my feet. My head jolted against the dashboard as the car lurched. Ahmed was still shouting profanities as he wrestled with the steering wheel, swaying from side to side. Then came the sound of automatic rifle fire, then the dull thuds as it hit the vehicle. I could see Ahmed's foot flat on the floor. I was thrown forward, sideways, backwards, up, and down as Ahmed tried to dodge the bullets. When the gunfire stopped, the vehicle slowed, then stopped. There was an eerie silence except for the sound of the engine running. *We've made it*, I thought, pulling myself up. I looked across at Ahmed, his forehead pressed firmly against the steering wheel, the bloody knife still in his hand. *Exhausted?*

I nudged him, and he groaned, "I've been hit; you drive, okay?"

"Ahmed, where? Let me see."

"My back."

"Let me look."

I shuffled across the seat; blood was soaking into his grey shirt, changing it from grey to deep brown.

"Ahmed, I need to have a closer look. Can you turn sideways so I can lift your shirt to see better?"

"No time, we must go now. You drive, okay?"

"Ahmed, I have to stop the bleeding now."

"No, we must drive fast; gunfire sounds travel far. You drive, don't argue."

"But we stop soon, okay."

"Okay. Now drive, please."

Ahmed shuffled across the front seats, and I exited the vehicle and changed places. I drove as fast as I could and stopped by a stretch of scrubland with no ruined buildings that could be a trap. I stopped the vehicle and walked around it, looking in every direction. I couldn't see anything except plastic bags floating in the breeze. I knew what I had to do and did it quickly. Ahmed was groaning with pain; I couldn't stop that, but I had to stem the blood oozing from his back. Our only clean rag was from the few clothes I hastily packed. I stuffed a cotton blouse into a cup of a bra. Then, I soaked it in perfume, hoping it had enough alcohol or something to disinfect the wound. Ahmed wasn't a big man, so luckily, with a bit of adjustment, it fitted well. I tightened his seat belt, so my makeshift dressing would pressurise the wound, pushing him firmly back against the seat, hopefully quelling the bleeding.

"Sorry, Ahmed, the only shirt I have left," I whispered as I dressed him in a lacy, flowery, feminine blouse. I don't think he heard, understood, or cared, as he was barely conscious. I drove the rest of the journey, slowly avoiding potholes. It was dusk. I could see well enough without using headlights. I kept nudging Ahmed, cajoling, "Stay awake, please."

He didn't say much other than grunt, "Inshallah."

At every road junction – luckily, there weren't many – I asked for directions. Ahmed tapped his right or left knee or pointed.

When we arrived at Jindires, I was surprised to be greeted by YPJ soldiers as though they were expecting us. We were frisked quickly and escorted by four female soldiers straight into the camp's first aid surgery. The medics swiftly treated Ahmed. Thanks to my improvised, spur-of-the-moment wound dressing, I had succeeded in stemming the blood flow. "Inshallah, he would survive," I was told.

I was informed later that a small recognisance group of YPJ soldiers happened to be close to the incident and heard gunfire. They saw the result of our incident: two rebels dead, and another one they quickly eradicated. They saw our vehicle in the distance, travelling at speed toward Jindires.

I was thoroughly searched before being taken to the officer in charge. She explained that Ali had been flown by an American helicopter in the first wave of the sick rescued from Raqqa. I would be put on the second wave. She was unsure when that would be and didn't know the extent of his illness, but he was in good hands. I was escorted by a female soldier to a room with a bed and told to rest. The soldier pointed to a shower and said, "If you want to." *A polite way of saying I wreaked?* She was correct; my clothes were covered in Ahmed's blood, desert dust and stunk of sweat. She spoke softly, "The canteen is open in a couple of hours. See you when you have freshened up."

The canteen diners were all young women dressed in the uniform of the YPJ, chattering in groups at the end of the day, as only women can. I was signalled to join them at their table and listened to their conversation. I didn't speak; I just watched and admired the soldiers in uniforms designed for men. How different they looked from the women in Aleppo. Some wore headscarves, and others had short hair, or it was tied back. Regardless of the slight difference in appearance, what struck me most was that they were all the same. Confident, smartly dressed, and athletic, the uniforms amplified their female form. In George's words, they didn't 'look like a bag of spanners', a phrase he used to say when observing women in men's clothes.

I butted in, "When will the next helicopter leave for Antalya?"

One of the soldiers replied, "Soon, and you will have company. Ahmed is coming with you."

I noticed the medic badge on the soldier who had replied, so I asked her, "Will he be okay?"

She replied, "The bullet is close to his spine; we can't remove it here." Giggling, she continued, "though we have been able to do something about his dress sense."

Ahmed, me, and others were flown to Antalya the following day. I was worried about Ali; I didn't sleep much that night.

On arrival at Antalya Hospital, Ahmed was met by a porter with a wheelchair and taken straight to the operation theatre suite. A nurse guided me into a side room, pointed to a person on a bed and told me he was my husband. *There has been a mistake; he must be somewhere else? Where is Ali?*

"Nurse, this isn't my husband."

"I think it is."

I looked at him again; it was nothing like his stature. The sheets clung to his skinny torso; where his skin was visible, it was bluish. Tubes and an oxygen mask covered most of his face.

This is not Ali. Why is she saying it is? "Sorry, nurse, you have made a mistake. Where is my husband?"

The nurse lifted the man's mask and indicated with her hand to get closer. *Why, for what?*

"Put your ear close to his mouth."

"Why?"

"Please do as I ask."

Why doesn't she listen? "Okay, to please you, but it wastes time."

Reluctantly, I did. I then heard a repeated whisper, barely audible. "Ali Mansour, Ali…"

I looked again; there was something familiar about his nose and forehead. *Could it be him?* I looked closer. No, this wasn't Ali. *Or was it?*

I awoke in a bed, almost touching another with that poor man lying on it. *What happened to me?* I studied the facial features to justify why the nurse told me it was Ali.

Then I remembered him whispering his name, so I imagined tracing Ali's forehead and nose down onto his lips like I used to, studying the profile beside me. I tried to move to get a better look and realised I was connected to a drip. *What are they doing to me?*

"Nurse, nurse, please, I need a nurse."

A nurse appeared at my bed; a thermometer was shoved in my mouth before I could speak. Her hand held my wrist as she looked at her upside-down watch.

"What can I do for you, Margaret?"

"Why am I in bed? Why the drip?"

"Okay, Margaret, you are in bed because you haven't been looking after yourself properly, have you?"

"Maybe, but why next to him."

"Your husband, you mean?"

"That's not my husband. There must be another Ali Mansour?"

"Why did you faint then?"

"I don't know, exhausted? Who knows?"

"Whatever you say. You will start to feel better soon."

"There is nothing wrong with me."

"Rest; I will bring you some food and drink."

I decided not to look at the poor man in the next bed.

After eating and drinking, I felt better and called the nurse. "Can I get out of bed and look for my husband?"

"Sure, I'll bring a chair over."

"I don't need a wheelchair; I can walk."

"I meant a chair so you can sit next to him."

"Bloody hell, how many times? It's not him."

"Okay, I'll get a chair."

The nurse placed a chair next to the other bed, helped me out of bed, steadied me with one arm, pushed the drip stand with the other, and sat me down in the comfortable chair. "Please look at him. It's not unusual in such cases to be in denial."

Denial? Bloody hell, does she think I don't know my own husband?

I looked at the poor man on the bed to appease the nurse. His breathing was shallow; he was so thin, nothing like Ali. His hair was similar; black and curly. Then I remembered tracing his forehead and looking at his nose a few minutes ago, dismissing the similarities.

"Nurse, nurse, please."

"Yes, Margaret, do you want something?"

"Can I see his hands, please?"

"Sorry, Margaret, they're both bandaged."

"My husband has a wedding ring that will prove it, once and for all."

"You think he would still be wearing it, knowing where he's been."

"Of course not."

"So why do you want to look at his hands."

"Because he had a copy of his wedding ring tattooed onto his ring finger after the war started, in case he was caught."

"Oh, I see." She cut the bandage away from the ring finger. "Like this, you mean?" The nurse held up his hand.

There it was. How could this be…?

I passed the chain from around my neck to the nurse and said, "See if it fits."

She removed the ring from the chain and gently slid it over the tattoo. "It's far too big."

"He will grow into it again, won't he?"

"Inshallah, I will tape it onto his finger."

I moved closer and held his hand. *What have they done to you?*

Chapter 15
Nursing Ali

I told my father that I was safe and with Ali in Antalya hospital, not disclosing the full details of Ali's condition. I would update him when I could understand what had happened to Ali. I begged my father to leave Syria and go somewhere safe. He promised he would, and he had somewhere in mind. He wouldn't say where but promised we would meet there one day. I asked him not to give me the answers or false promises or tell me what I wanted to hear. I wanted nothing but to be told the truth.

I leaned over by the side of the bed and whispered into Ali's ear, "It's Margaret. Can you hear me?" No reply. *How could this be Ali?*

The nurse returned. "Margaret, please, don't try and wake him. He's in an induced coma," she said tetchily.

"Why? Coma?"

"Because he will heal better. It takes time."

"How long?"

"It depends on how he reacts to the meds and nutrients."

"He is going to be okay?"

"He is in excellent hands. The doctors know what they are doing."

"Okay. Are there many others like him?"

"Unfortunately, he is one of the few that made it."

"It is Ali? We are absolutely sure?" *Why do I need reassurance?*

"Absolutely. When he arrived, delirious, he whispered, 'Margaret, wait for me'. Not a popular name in Syria."

"What have they done to him?"

"Now is not the time for that."

"How long do you think before he knows I am here?"

"As I said, it takes time, but a few weeks maybe; who knows?"

I slowly came to terms with the fact that the poor man was Ali. The days rolled into weeks. His skin colour changed, and he gained weight. There were periods of rapid eye movement accompanied by a fever. I smoothed his brow with ice packs. Eventually, the doctors decided it was time to reduce the drug dose of pentobarbital and bring him out of his coma.

On the big day, I was encouraged to talk to and touch him as much as possible. Though he might be confused, hearing my voice and feeling my touch could help. As Ali emerged from the coma, he seemed alarmed, confused, and agitated. The doctors expected this to happen as he hallucinated before being put into a controlled coma. His brain had to slowly process where he was and what was happening to him.

He kept asking, "Are we in the other place?"

I knew Ali didn't believe there was such a thing, *so why was he asking?*

After a temporary hearing device was fitted, he slowly understood where he was but didn't understand why. I assured him he was in the best place and would soon be his old self again.

When his oxygen mask was removed, I could see the full extent of the beatings his face had taken. His strong chin was sunken, and perfect teeth were no longer visible. Scars covered his face where he had been bludgeoned with something hard. His speech was difficult to understand, as he wasn't controlling his mouth. The doctor explained that his jaw might have been smashed, and the bone had reset crookedly. It was cosmetic and would be fixed in time, and that was the least of their worries. The doctors continued to sedate him to relieve pain and restrict movement. He drifted in and out of consciousness and frequently woke in distress, tossing his head from side to side. Sometimes, he screamed his name. Sometimes, his body was rigid, with his face grimacing. When fully awake, he became agitated when the nurses wouldn't give him a mirror. I watched him run his tongue around his mouth, confused and asking what had happened. The nurses told me to placate him by telling him 'all in good time'.

The doctor treating Ali explained that treatment options for patients suffering from PTSD after torture may include therapy, medication, and other forms of treatment. He would prepare a dossier for the hospital in the UK that would be taking over the rehabilitation. He went on to say that developing coping strategies, such as relaxation and stress-management techniques, helped manage symptoms of PTSD. He emphasised that recovery was a protracted process. Proper support would enable the management of symptoms and improve quality of life. As soon as Ali was well enough, arrangements were made with Frimley Hospital in the UK, which specialises in PTSD suffered mainly by members of the armed forces.

Concerned about Ahmed, I visited him to check on his recovery and thank him for his bravery. He had recovered sufficiently to be discharged. Luckily, the bullet lodged close to his spine but didn't put pressure on his spinal cord. The operation was uncomplicated, and his total recovery would be swift. He asked about Ali and if he could see him. Ali was often asleep, so I chose a time when that was so. I didn't want Ali to see his friend's face when he saw him, and I wasn't sure how Ahmed would react. I saw the disbelief on Ahmed's face as his head shook from side to side, looking at me, indicating he couldn't believe it was Ali. Or maybe he couldn't think that another human could do this to another. I nodded to confirm it was Ali. Ahmed copied my nod, then opened his hands before him, silently asking, 'Why?'. I shook my head, indicating I didn't know how someone could do this. The tears rolling down Ahmed's cheeks caused a deluge in me, and I cried openly for the first time. We embraced as mourners do, witnessing the loss of someone who is loved dearly.

I asked Ahmed, "What about you? Where will you go?"

With a puzzled look, he replied, "Aleppo inshallah."

"Ahmed, haven't you done enough?"

"I have nowhere else to go; my family are there."

"Are they well? Can you get them to safety?"

"They will always be in Aleppo."

"Do you have a wife and children? If so, get them out now, please."

"They can never leave Aleppo, you understand?"

"Oh."

"We will all be in the same place soon, inshallah."

I understood comradeship at that moment. Ali used to say standing shoulder to shoulder, knowing that the man standing next to you will put his body on the line to protect yours, forms a special bond. I felt that way about Ahmed; although we had just met, what we had been through together had formed that bond. Just as Ali didn't want to leave his comrades behind in Aleppo, I didn't want to break the bond Ahmed and I had formed. To Ahmed, I was just one of many. He had a duty to his friends in Aleppo, so I wished him well, knowing I would never see him again or learn how his life would pan out.

Chapter 16

Back in the UK

Assisted boarding from Antalya to Heathrow Airport made the journey doable. Ali could stand alone and walk short distances, so the physical part wasn't a problem. I was concerned about mixing in crowds and how he would cope with the airport's hustle and bustle. Ali had asked me not to tell any of our friends in the UK where we were. I told Allan and Amina we were coming to the UK against Ali's wishes, insisting they didn't try to meet us. Ali wasn't ready to see any of our friends yet. We were still in contact with George Newall, who remained a good friend despite my initial misgivings. I felt our closest friends should know we were safe. But Ali insisted he wasn't ready to meet people he knew before.

Walking into the arrival lounge, I spotted Allan and Amina; I hoped they wouldn't be there. Amina promised they wouldn't, but they were. I couldn't blame them; I would have probably done the same thing. When they saw me, I noticed by their expressions they were confused. *Was it because I had changed so much? Or were their eyes searching for Ali, who was taller than me.* I assumed they were looking for him, so I glanced at the porter pushing the wheelchair and smiled. They followed my glance to the wheelchair. I saw the shock on their faces as they realised the person in the wheelchair was Ali. They both held the other's hand for support and then ran to greet us as fast as possible.

"Sorry, Ali."

Ali mumbled, "What the fuck?"

Ali's hearing had deteriorated. The temporary fix had failed, and he was now almost totally deaf. I watched as Allan tried to talk to him, and Ali turned away, trying to hide what had been done to him, as pity was the last thing he needed.

I made the greeting as short as possible, as I could see Ali struggling to cope with everything around him. I said goodbye to them, explaining that Ali was going to Frimley Hospital for treatment and I would keep them up to date. It was best our meeting was short. The shock on their faces wasn't good for Ali or me.

Ali settled into the treatment programme his array of doctors had decided upon. I kept Allan and Amina updated on Ali's recovery; though slow, it was progressing.

I contacted George, guilty I didn't let him know where we were sooner. It had been a while since we spoke, and I could no longer hide the truth from him. George was very astute and could see through my fictional account, which didn't match the UK news about Aleppo. He assumed we were still there, so he was surprised we were back in the UK and wanted to see us both soon. I didn't tell George the full extent of Ali's injuries, only about his recovery. I insisted he wouldn't be able to visit Ali until he was better. George decided that he wanted to see us regardless of what I wanted.

I hadn't seen George for years; he occasionally updated us on his career. Despite what we thought was a misspent youth, George was exceptionally bright; everything seemed easy, and he excelled at his studies. We often joked that the female visitors to his rooms were case studies. He returned the joke by saying that bringing work home was his route to success, and it was backbreaking work and not fun. It was a duty, not a pleasure; somebody had to put in the hard yards, so it might as well be him. In a way, he was correct. He certainly had a large circle of friends, both male and female.

After obtaining a first-class degree in psychology, he changed course slightly and received a first in psychiatry. So, when George turned up at Frimley visitors' lounge, it wasn't a surprise. He always did things his way. But seeing the change in George after all the years was a surprise. I pictured him as he was during his misspent youth, the charming hippie that girls found attractive. Instead, a tall, slim, distinguished, smartly dressed man stood before me. Gone was the curly hair cascading onto his shoulders, replaced with a neat ponytail. His spotty white face was now tanned, and a trim, manicured goatee beard adorned his chin. He looked like a psychiatrist, like the pictures on the front of books or celebrities on television.

George's manner hadn't changed. I remembered what Ali said about him. "He takes time to listen and is thoughtful in his replies." He did precisely that; he let me talk and talk about old times. Whenever he said something, his words were few and precise. Then he said, "Let's talk about you."

"There's nothing to tell."

"Margaret, your eyes and body language tell me a lot."

"I am so worried about Ali; what was done to him, I don't think he will fully recover."

"Margaret, I want to talk about you; Ali is being treated. What about you?"

"Nothing to tell, really."

"Margaret, I know what happened to Ali, and the treatment he is getting here is best."

"How? Who told you?"

"Ali's psychologist told me."

"Is that allowed? Confidentiality and all that."

"You're correct. Of course, they told me enough, but they were also concerned about you."

"There's nothing to tell, George, so stop bloody asking."

"Margaret, in the short time we have been talking, I can tell something has changed in you."

"Such as?"

"You would have swotted away my questions with some witty remarks. Now you are on the defensive instead of the attack; words like 'nothing to tell', that is not you. You would have responded with a sarcastic remark or innuendo to deflect my questions, with a smirk on your face."

"Bloody hell, George, I have been through a war. What do you expect?"

"At last, we are getting somewhere."

"George, please, I want to forget the horrors; you have no idea."

"Margaret, sooner or later, you must come to terms with what you have seen; that is the best way. Opening up and talking about it won't make it disappear, but there are ways of coping with it."

"Not now, George. I have other things on my mind."

"Is there anyone you can talk to?"

"Not really. I don't want to burden anyone."

"I understand. Sometimes, it's best to talk to a stranger. I could arrange that when you are ready."

"Maybe, but I need to concentrate on Ali first."

"You can concentrate on Ali better if you are in a better place."

"Please, George, not now."

"Sorry, I didn't mean to press you. I just want to help."

"I know, George, but I don't want Ali to discover what happened to me. He would never be able to forgive himself."

"I understand that, but if you can't come to terms with it, it will always be a barrier between you both."

"When Ali gets better, we will talk. Now drop it, please."

"Margaret, what if he doesn't get much better? What then?"

"George, for fuck's sake, I was raped. There. Now, leave it."

"I thought it must have been something like that."

"That's not all, George. I've seen so much suffering. I don't want the memories flooding back."

"I know you want to forget, but when you are ready, I can arrange for you to receive treatment."

"Okay, when I'm ready, but not now, okay."

"Fine, just to let you know, people respond to different treatments. You must receive a proper assessment and care from trained professionals; I can arrange that when you are ready, okay?"

"Whatever, George, but not now."

"Just one more thing. Are you on any medication?"

"Just the normal stuff, vitamins, iron tablets, that sort of thing."

"I'll have a word with your doctor here. See what he thinks."

"I don't need any medication. I am not ill."

"I'll have a word anyway; antidepressants might help."

"Ali said you didn't say much; you've certainly changed."

"Other things can be done to help, like cognitive behavioural therapy or eye movement desensitisation and reprocessing."

"George, you're just showing off now; enough, okay?"

"Just one more thing, well, two really. Knowing you, I think you would be more suited to either group or exposure therapy."

"Okay, George, whatever, can we talk of something else? Is there 'something else therapy'? I could settle for that? Don't answer. I'm brain dead."

"Almost back to your old self, then, touché."

"George, can we talk of other things over a glass of red wine somewhere lovely. Maybe we can talk about what a prat you were. That would take my mind somewhere else. For instance, who are you shagging? Have you settled down? Have you found Mrs Right? I could go on, anything but Ali or me."

"Yes, of course. What about taking you from this place to somewhere nice, my treat."

"That would mean putting on a bit of slap. I can't go looking like this."

"You look fine, but whatever. I can call back this evening and collect you."

"Okay, George, can you pick me up from the Travelodge around the corner?"

"Done. See you later then, about seven o'clock, okay."

After George left, I asked one of the young female nurses if she had any make-up I could borrow. She gave me a bag and said, "Take your pick."

Sitting in front of a mirror at the Travelodge for the first time in ages, I saw what I had become. *No amount of make-up will fix this; look at my hair.* I combed it through and plonked it on top of my head. In the mirror, I saw Ali standing behind me; the memory was as if it had happened only yesterday. I had taken ages getting ready. We were going somewhere special. Ali leant and kissed my right shoulder, and slowly, his lips moved up my neck, and then he gently nipped my ear. Looking at him through the mirror, I pointed to my left shoulder and leaned slightly so he could repeat what he had just done.

I said, "Are you sure you want to go out?" He started to undo his tie, still gazing at me in the mirror. Then I said, "Only joking." And watched the disappointment on his face as he readjusted his tie.

Shit, mascara was running in streaks down my face. I hadn't cried over happy times for such a long time. *Get yourself together, girl.*

George collected me in a bright red little sports car. *Not what the old George would have gone for.* I clambered into the passenger seat, avoiding rearranging my hair precariously piled on my head. The restaurant George selected was not what the old George would have chosen. There was no real ale on tap here; beer, if any, came in small, expensive bottles with inflated prices. It was quiet, unlike a rowdy pub I wrongly assumed would have been George's choice. We were shown to a secluded corner where I didn't feel underdressed and could talk to each other without shouting.

"So, George, tell me about yourself. You've done very well, it seems. Do you have a partner, or are you still trying to shag the whole UK?"

"I have a partner – just the one. We met in Paris at a convention."

"Not satisfied with trying to shag the whole of the UK, you thought to give the common market a go? What does she do? Does she have a name?"

"She is a psychiatrist like me; her name is written H-u-a and pronounced 'khwah'."

"That's not very French, is it?"

"No, she's Chinese. She's in London, and we share a flat."

"Bloody hell, George, Europe wasn't big enough for your portfolio, so you decided to take on the world."

"It wasn't like that. She seduced me, in fact."

"George, they all did."

"I couldn't help it if girls found me attractive."

"Really, George, you thought the girls were attracted to you?" *Which they were.* "None of them stuck around, though, did they?"

"No, they were all out for a good time, no strings."

"George, it was a 'rite of passage' for the girls. It was sort of a club, those that had shagged you and those that hadn't."

George looked sullen; *have I damaged his ego?* So, I told him the truth. "Sorry, George, I was just playing with you. They all loved you, well, almost all."

"You had me going then, didn't you?"

"I thought you were a prat, and you thought I was one to avoid."

George proudly showed me photos of his latest conquest. I was surprised at his choice. She wasn't amazingly beautiful; her eyes were typically Asian, her face round with small features. I asked, "Is this one a keeper."

"Never been so sure; she's amazing." His expression proved to me there was no doubt.

"Wedding bells ringing soon, then?"

"Maybe, hopefully, if she will have me."

Sitting close to George brought back memories of the night Ali, and I almost stayed in. The memory of getting ready to go out with Ali still lingered. We were dining out with George and his latest conquest, the four of us chatting. I could see in Ali's eyes he wished we had stayed home. I removed one of my shoes and playfully tucked my foot inside his trouser leg, stroking his shin. I couldn't help laughing as Ali tried to continue his conversation while obviously aroused. When we got home, he removed my coat, kissed my neck, scooped me up, and carried me into the bedroom. Afterwards, he said, "That wasn't half bad, was it?"

I chuckled at my memory. George asked, "What's up? Have I said something funny?"

I wasn't listening to George's ramblings, so I said, "Sorry, a lovely memory of Ali just popped into my head."

"It must have been amusing; here, wipe your eyes. The waiters will think it's me who made you cry."

I hadn't talked to anyone for a long time. George was a good listener. I had kept so much locked up inside.

Once I opened up, everything tumbled out. It spilt out in no particular order. I rambled on about Ali and me. "When he did manage to get away from the White Helmets, it was a relief for both of us. We never really talked, didn't make love, or slept like spoons anymore. We were like zombies, living but not alive, going through the motions of life." All the emotions hidden deep inside that I was frightened to release flooded out of me. I didn't want to spend another second locked in that world… "Thanks for listening, George; you're not such a prat after all."

I hadn't thought about the words which I blurted out to George. I was shocked when I heard myself pleading with George, "Can I stay the night with you, please, George?" *Was it the wine that was breaking the log jam of emotion?*

George was watching my face with an expression of disbelief and asked, "Why?"

"Jesus, George, you're the psychiatrist; tell me why?" George didn't answer. "George, I need to be with someone who knows me, cares, that's all."

"Okay, you can stay with me if it helps. I'll get the bill."

I could feel the tears of relief running down my cheeks. "Thanks, George. I need to go to the toilet to clean up. I must look like something on Halloween night."

George was waiting for me, standing beside the maître d'. I could see the concern on George's face. *Am I doing the right thing?* We didn't talk on the way to George's hotel other than small talk about the meal we had just eaten.

When we entered George's hotel room, he pointed to the bathroom, saying, "I'll get you a clean shirt. Is that okay? There's a complimentary toothbrush. Anything else?"

"Fine, George." I noticed a double bed in the room. Sorry, "I thought there would be two separate beds."

"No problem, I'll sleep on the floor."

"No, you won't, George, I will."

"Okay, there is a solution. You have the duvet, and I'll have the sheet," George said, folding the duvet and sheet in half. "That way, we have our own sleeping zones."

I nodded at the bedding arrangement. "That'll work."

I turned out the light and snuggled into my duvet. "Goodnight, George."

"Sleep tight, Margaret."

I slept well; maybe the wine? I awoke in the middle of the night, hugging Ali; we were like spoons again. I felt warm and secure like it used to be. I pulled his shoulder so he would turn and face me. "Are you sure?" a voice barely audible said.

"Please, help me forget."

I knew by then it was George, but it didn't matter; I needed to feel someone, anyone. I needed to escape. It didn't matter who it was. I wanted to make love and feel excited and alive again. George turned, aroused. I felt his body, not Ali's, but it was Ali's. I didn't care; it didn't matter. I needed to feel like a woman again and experience pleasure and love.

Afterwards, still holding each other, I whispered, "Sorry, George, I needed to feel human again."

"No need, I understand, and I wanted to help."

"I didn't plan this, George. It just happened; you know that?"

"Of course, just therapy. It's our secret. You're not my type anyway." He chuckled. "Coffee?"

"In a minute. Can you hold me a little longer? Remember, I'm the ice maiden... George, you took a long time to answer when I asked if I could stay here tonight. Ali told me you always thought things through. What were you thinking about? Did you think about Hua?"

"I was thinking about what would happen, and Hua never came into it."

"You mean you knew we would end up like this?"

"No, that was not it; I know what you think of me, the way I treated women. I used them and moved on. It was not like that at all. Well, from your point of view, it was just like that, but it wasn't. I'm with Hua because she understood that from the outset. With her, it is different. I told her everything because I wanted to. I didn't want a one-night stand. I didn't want to lose her, so I told her the truth."

"So, what is the truth, George? Can you share it with me?"

"No, not yet, maybe one day. Something traumatic happened to me as a child; don't ask. Hua is the only person who found the truth, the only one I could tell because I needed her to know. Hua understood my behaviour was compensating for what was missing from my childhood. Perhaps you understand now, after last night. You felt you needed to be with someone. It didn't matter who; your subconscious knew you needed a respite. A bit like a computer needs to get rid of bad histories and cookies if you like and do a system reset."

I quipped, "That's one way of putting it. I think my hard drive is corrupted with a virus now."

"I know you thought I was a prat, shagging women like it was some sort of challenge. Well, it wasn't like that. I hope now you will understand me. What happened to you last night, the feelings you had. The yearning to be close to someone, hold another person and feel their body's warmth against yours. Escape from real life into a dream world where nothing is wrong, no evil, no pain, just pleasure. That's what I was doing, being a selfish prat. Escape was all I wanted; it wasn't about sex or lust. So, I knew that was what you wanted, sorry, needed. Could I be that person? Could I walk away and treat the encounter as frivolous as I used to? So, Margaret, that's what I was thinking. This morning, I am glad it was me. It was the first time I had slept with someone who needed to escape as much as me."

"George, thank you for being a selfish prat like me."

"No problem, just another notch on my bedpost."

"I'd love that coffee now, George. As the saying goes, what happens between the sheets stays there, okay?"

"Let's just say we were good therapy for each other. Sugar? How many?"

"Just black, thanks, George. Now you've seen my issues at close quarters, what is your professional opinion, Doctor? You are a doctor, yes?"

"Yes, I am a doctor, well, a professor, but I am still George to you."

"Okay, Prof, what do you recommend?"

"It's George. I can't advise you after last night. It wouldn't be ethical or prudent to prescribe treatment. Regardless of last night, you are a close friend, so the best option is to see someone with fresh eyes. Will you be able to tell Ali about the rape?"

"No, never, not because he would think wrong of me, but because he would blame himself."

"What about our therapy last night? Will you tell him?"

"No, I could never tell him because he wouldn't understand."

"Do you feel guilty about last night?"

"No, I don't yet. Will I? I don't know because Ali is the only man I've slept with till now. George, do you regret it?"

"No, but I won't tell Hua, though she would understand. It might be an issue for you when you meet her."

"So, George, where do I go from here? In your professional opinion?"

"Well, I think you should give group therapy a go."

"But that's about people spouting about all the bad things that have happened to them, isn't it?"

"You are looking at it from an opposing point of view. It's surprising the benefit of releasing pent-up emotions. Relating your experience to others and them being prepared to listen and not judge you will help. Your reward for listening to others and not judging will surprise you. Your inward emotions dissipate when you fully understand what others have experienced."

"I am still unsure about therapy. Will Ali be offered something similar?"

"Probably. I can't say which treatment. Where Ali is, they have trained therapists or licensed mental health professionals; they're the experts in PTSD."

"Okay, I'll think about therapy, promise."

"As far as you're concerned, I think you will benefit from being part of a group. You will learn that you are not alone; others have experienced similar struggles. This will help to reduce your feelings of isolation, shame, and self-blame. If it works for you, you will develop a sense of community and support from others who understand what you are going through. Learning you are not alone and being in a group normalises your feelings and reduces the shame. Please, Margaret, give it a try; what have you got to lose?"

"Okay, Prof, I will try. Can you take me back to the hospital, please? I need to see Ali and come back into reality."

Walking from George's car to the hospital in the crisp fresh air, I realised it was spring; daffodils and crocuses were starting to bloom, carpeting the entrance. *Were they here yesterday?* I turned to George. "One more thing, George, hold me tight, squeeze me." When I let George stop squeezing me, I pulled away and said, "George, Hua is a fortunate woman; how wrong I was about you. Thank you for the therapy; you've turned out to be some doctor; just one course of treatment, and I feel much better."

George smiled. "Wait until you see the bill."

As George returned to the car, I waved goodbye and shouted, "Love you, Professor Newall."

He waved back. "Love you, Mrs Mansour."

The respite was over; I felt different somehow, more optimistic that Ali would get better. I hadn't been told the full extent of Ali's injuries yet; they said they were many, so assessing him would take time. Most physical stuff, like his blood and nutrition, were straightforward to monitor. The other things, like broken bones, would take time as they had to be reset, but they weren't a primary concern either. The psychological stuff would take longer, and the outcome would be unsure. I was constantly made aware of this by the doctors.

The doctor treating Ali spotted and greeted me as I entered the ward. "Could you come into the office, please, Mrs Mansour? I am Doctor Phillips; please call me David. I will be the lead doctor looking after Ali."

I offered my hand, and he shook it warmly as I asked him, "How is he doing?"

"Coming along slowly, but I want you to sit down; I have unwelcome news. Sorry for being blunt; Ali will never father a child."

"Oh, I see."

"I can understand the shock. I believe you have no children yet?"

"No, we don't, but what have they done to him?"

"Sorry, I don't know the details. All I can tell you is that the bastards used something mechanical on his reproductive organs: tongs, pliers, hammers, or something."

"So, do you mean they have removed them?"

"No, fortunately, they're just mangled, but as far as a sexual organ, it won't function, you see."

"Oh, does he know?"

"No, not yet; it would possibly cause a setback if he were to find out now. So it's best to keep him optimistic for the future. We can get the other things out of the way, like his hearing, which technology can improve, and his mouth – again, purely cosmetic. Then we have to concentrate on everything else they have done to him. That's the tricky bit; at the moment, he has no conscious recollection of what they did. His brain couldn't cope, so it shut down. Like me, you probably noticed his subconscious is coming to the surface. He has rapid eye movements and cold sweats. He wakes up startled, drops off to sleep, and wakes up minutes later confused."

"Yes, I've seen all that; when he wakes, it's like he's somewhere else. He thought we were both in heaven or limbo. I wasn't sure which, as he didn't believe in either. He does know now he is in hospital, though still confused how he got here."

"Yes, he understands now, knows I am his doctor. So now, the intensive therapy begins. We are unsure how he will cope with what they did to him when or if his memory returns. Judging how much medication will be required to keep him calm will be trial and error. I have seen others like Ali lash out at those tending them, so they must be restrained for their safety and others."

"I have a psychiatrist friend; he said he is in the best place."

"You mean Professor George Newall?"

"Yes, do you know him?"

"No, not really. He's been on the phone a lot, asking questions."

"Sorry about that, but he is a close friend of Ali."

"No need to apologise; he was enquiring, that's all."

"George advised me about different therapies; when will they decide which? When will they start?"

"Soon. The PTSD team will decide when he is ready. It's up to them; they take the lead in his mental health. Do you require any counselling? You must have witnessed some awful things."

"What has George told you?"

"Nothing at all, except for what I just said."

"Maybe I will later; let's concentrate on Ali first."

"Ali is waiting for you. He has already asked where you are. If there is anything else, just ask."

Ali was sitting up in bed waiting for me. He smiled. *It's not the same smile without his flashing white teeth.* I smiled back and kissed his cheek.

He asked me, "You okay? You seem worried."

I mouthed, "Sorry, George dropped in to see me."

Ali looked confused, so I spelt 'George Newall' on his forearm using my index finger.

Ali grinned, saying, "How is he? Has he changed much?"

I related everything George had told me about himself as best I could. Surprisingly, I felt no guilt for leaning on George for comfort. *Maybe that'll come later.*

The tests on the most effective device to repair Ali's hearing narrowed to a cochlear implant or a bone-anchored hearing aid. There were positive and negative impacts for each. The audiologists decided that a bone-anchored hearing aid would give the best results. The drawback was that it was not as discreet as an implant and clearly visible to others. This might be another reminder to Ali, but being able to hear better outweighed any reservations.

After the hearing device was fitted, I could finally talk with Ali again. The more we talked, the more questions Ali asked, and then the fog slowly lifted from his brain. He became angry at everyone and everything; he didn't sleep unless he was dosed with sleeping pills and antidepressants. During sleep, he screamed his name, curled up in a ball, hands tight to his head as though protecting himself. Other times, he lay flat and rigid, his face distorted as though combating some awful pain.

Several male nurses restrained him when he uncurled and thrashed about. I was ushered out of the room as a doctor approached with a needle to inject him with something.

Doctor Phillips called me into his office to explain the therapy was about to start. It was trial and error as to which treatment would suit. The PTSD team decided on behavioural therapy. I was told it might be better not to witness the treatment, as he could see how Ali's outbursts affected me. Ali's notes from the team in Antalya contained notes about their concerns for me, concluding that I had experienced some sort of trauma. *So, it wasn't just George that was concerned.*

The doctor asked, "Would it help to talk about it? If so, you could be referred to the psychotherapy team."

"As I said, I have had some bad experiences, but Ali comes first."

"No, you come first; Ali will need you. He will push your love and resolve to the limit. You need to be up to the task."

"No, Ali comes first. I will cope with everything."

"I have seen so many wives like you, trying to cope and failing."

"You never knew Ali before. He will come through this; he's a fighter."

"Okay, have it your way, but you need a break. Is there anywhere you can go? Be with friends for a brief time?"

"Yes, I have friends, but I want to stay."

"I want you to go, please, for yours and Ali's sake. It will benefit both. Go and spend some time with your friends, please."

"I'll think about it, but I should be here with Ali."

"Okay, but we may have to deny you access, for both your sakes."

Is he only saying this to make sure I go? Why?

Allan and Amina had said several times I could spend time with them in Pembroke. So, I decided to accept the offer. They insisted that they would journey to the hospital and drive me back to their home. On the journey to Pembroke, Allan was at the wheel, and Amina and I sat in the back of the car. I had nothing to say but listened to them prattle on about everyday things. I had forgotten how different my life had been since they left Aleppo. *They have no idea what it was like. Words can't describe the things that Ali and I saw.* Without thinking, I told them about the horrors I had seen. I cried openly. It didn't matter. I didn't care what they thought about me. Maybe it was their inane chattering because they didn't know what to say to me. Triggered by the stark difference between their life and mine, I wanted to shock them into my world. Amina repeated there was no need, but I couldn't stop. I wasn't talking to them. I was talking to myself. I felt relief. *Is it because someone else knows what I've been through? Unloading onto others lessens my load. Does therapy work?* I didn't tell them everything, some things they would never know. *Strange, I could tell George about the rape, but not my closest friends?* They didn't say much for the rest of the journey, *careful not to cause another outburst? Or shock?*

Amara and Amal were there to meet us. How they had grown. Amara was a carbon copy of her mother. Amal was a mixture of both parents but was now taller than Amina and Amara. They were no longer little children but young adults; they had changed so much. *Have I, too?*

We talked about the good times. Can you remember this or that and general chatter. *Strangely, Ali never enquired about the kids.*

Amina took me shopping and to the hairdresser to cheer me up. I kept in touch with Doctor Phillips for feedback on Ali's progress and was told there was a slight improvement, and the therapy was beginning to work.

Chapter 17

With Baba at Last

Baba phoned me while I was still at Allan and Amina's house, which was a pleasant surprise. I took the phone call to another room so no one else could hear. His first words were, "Is it safe to talk?"

"Yes, Baba, I am on my own."

"Good, please don't tell anyone else; I'm in England."

"England...? How come?"

"It's a long story. Can we meet somewhere?"

"I'm in Pembroke, staying with Allan and Amina."

"Is Ali there too?"

"No, he is in hospital having therapy."

"Why aren't you with him?"

"I'll tell you when we meet, it's a long story."

"When are you coming back to Frimley?"

"I haven't made any plans. But it could be a while; I'm waiting for the doctor to let me know."

"Oh, I see."

We both came up with the exact words, "Why don't we meet in Pembroke?" We agreed it was a great idea.

"Can you keep it as our little secret?"

"Don't worry, Baba, I won't tell anyone."

"I will ring you tomorrow when I have made the arrangements; I can't wait to see you."

"Me too, Baba; love you."

"Love you too."

"Who was that on the phone?" Amina asked, possibly thinking it was news about Ali.

"Ali's doctor, just an update, slight improvement, the same as usual." *How can I meet my father without Allan and Amina knowing? I need a plan.*

My father phoned the following day and told me his plans. He rented a cottage for a few weeks close to Freshwater East; he hired a car so we could meet anywhere. I planned to tell the James family I was going back to Frimley by train. I knew they would insist on taking me there by car. I argued their logic of driving all the way there and back when I could get there faster by train didn't make any sense. They would have to take time off work, so they agreed reluctantly.

I planned to board the train at Pembroke and get off at Lamphey, the next stop. My father would be waiting for me and take me to the cottage, which was nearby at Freshwater East. It worked like clockwork; I met my father at Lamphey station. He greeted me with hugs and kisses and told me how well I looked, and I did the same. *I was telling a half-truth; was he too?* I could see a change; he was gaunter, his hair thinner and peppered with more grey streaks, but still a handsome man.

Once settled in the rented cottage, I asked my father, "What are you doing in England, Baba?"

"Because I had to get out, even though I was a minister in the government, I wasn't one of them. Sooner rather than later, they would find out. The punishment would be execution as a traitor."

"So you knew they suspected you?"

"No, not really, until I was told, thankfully, by someone who could help me."

"And who could that be? Can I guess? Fatima, wasn't it."

"Yes, it was Fatima."

"So, what did she do?"

"Worked her magic, slowed down the dossier on me getting anywhere."

"You mean conveniently she lost it."

"Or slowed it down. I don't know; she then arranged a route to an asylum camp in Türkiye with all the correct paperwork."

"Is she putting herself at risk?"

"She says no."

"Do you believe her?"

"Yes, after the civil war started, we saw more of each other. I came to terms with what she did. I never forgave her, though."

"Baba, first I hated her, then felt sorry for her."

"Enough, Margaret, time for bed. Let us talk tomorrow; I have something planned. Hopefully, the weather is fine. You know what it's like in Pembrokeshire; it has a mind of its own."

"Goodnight, Baba; looking forward to my surprise tomorrow."

We were up early for breakfast as we drove to our mystery destination, which I thought would be Barafundle Bay. I tried to look surprised when we pulled into Stackpole Quay car park.

"This is a walk down memory lane for me," Baba said as he held out his hand.

"Me too," I replied, holding and squeezing his hand.

I remembered the walk over the headland to the beautiful isolated Barafundle Bay as a child. Judged by experts to be one of the most picturesque views in the world, who could disagree? We didn't talk. Like me, I assumed that my father was consumed with memories of my mother. My father found the exact same spot I used to sit with her. We sat and admired the view; being spring, there were not many brave swimmers, just the odd one. Probably a local who braved the cold sea in reverence to it. Children and pet dogs chased the tide in and out, some being outwitted by the occasional wave catching them out as they looked to their parents for help. We couldn't hear the squeals of delight above the noise of the wind or the sea.

Then my father started to talk. "This brings back so many memories. This is the place I promised your mother that I would return for her one day. I blamed Fatima for intercepting our letters. It wasn't Fatima's fault. I should have found out why she wasn't replying. I should have come back as promised. I should have realised something was wrong. Why didn't I? I have thought hard about my reasoning recently. Why didn't I do anything? Maybe subconsciously, my psyche assumed that anyone I loved would do the same. That's why there has never been anyone in my life else since your mother."

"It was long ago, Baba; perhaps my mother could have tried harder."

"Fatima and I were so much in love. She pushed me away when she found out she couldn't have children.

I still loved her for so long, hoping her love for me would return. But it didn't."

"Baba, I can understand. I know how you feel now. Maybe we are more alike than you think. Ali has been the only person I have ever loved. But when the person changes into someone else you don't even like, how is it possible to stay in love with them."

"You and Ali are nothing like Fatima and me. Your love will endure; it's so strong, you have nothing to worry about."

"Baba, I am really struggling. It's not because Ali's appearance has changed, his injuries or his physicality, or what has been done to him that affects me. I fell in love with his personality; take away that, and he is no longer Ali. If he becomes someone else, I don't know if I can love him. I can care for him, nurse him and love him as another human, but I can't love him as a wife. Just like you loved Fatima with all your heart until she changed."

"I still have memories of Fatima when we were young and so in love. I knew she wanted a child more than me. When I learned about you, I knew she wanted a child, hers and mine created between us. Discovering I fathered a child, she substituted you as her own. She thought telling me the truth would take you from her. I think that's why she kept you a secret. Did she push me away because she had you? I don't know. It's still a mystery to me. I wanted us to have a child, but I wanted her more."

"But it was all an illusion to Fatima. I knew nothing about her, so I can't love her as a daughter should."

"I know, the human mind is a mystery to me, even more complicated when it's female."

"Some call it a 'ticking clock', the timing mechanism a contrivance for child production. It throws a wobbly when that doesn't happen."

"Are you likely to throw a wobbly?"

"No, I have godchildren. I'm a surrogate mother to them."

"When I met your mother, she blew me away; she knew I was married and believed me when I told her my marriage was over and I would return one day. We promised to write as often as we could. Well, you know the rest."

"Oh, Baba, imagine how different it would have been."

"Yes, it would."

"I did the same as Fatima when I realised I couldn't bear Ali's child. I pushed him away, and Ali worked hard to convince me it didn't matter. Ali, though, had help from his friend, George, who I thought was a right prat."

"What did his friend do?

"He listened. You would have to meet him to understand that he listens and thinks and doesn't open his mouth until he's sure his advice will help."

"I never had a friend like that. Pity, but if I had, maybe you wouldn't be here, and we wouldn't be having this conversation."

"Maybe. That's life, as they say. Who knows how things pan out in the end."

"What does this thinking man do for a living?"

"George is now an eminent psychiatrist."

"Now, that is no surprise. Do you see him much now?"

"No, not so much. Baba, you were also living in a different time and culture, so different from today.

For instance, you accepted Ali and me into your home and offered us a room to share even though you knew we were not married. Would that have happened in your time? Would your parents have done the same thing?"

"No, most definitely not. Different time, different people."

My father drove me back to his place in London, a rented apartment that suited him as it was easy to keep a low profile. The following day, he drove me to Frimley Hospital. He wanted to see Ali. I told him it wasn't possible, and he seemed highly disappointed. No amount of telling people how unwell Ali was would make them understand. *Why does everyone think they are unique? Seeing Ali would give him a boost? It's the opposite. He would rather old friends remember him as he was, not as he is now.* So, when my father left, it was with a promise that he could see Ali next time.

Ali was sitting in bed; he looked better to me physically, though his eyes looked tired. I kissed his cheek in the usual manner.

With a raised, angry voice, he asked, "Where have you been?"

"You don't remember? I said I was spending a little time with Alan and Amina."

"Yes, I remember that; that's not what I asked you."

"I was with Allan and Amina."

"Don't lie to me."

Why is he so angry? "I am not lying."

"Yes, you bloody well are; they rang looking for you."

"Allan and Amina? When was that?"

"Last week."

"Oh, I was with my father then."

"What, in Damascus? Do you think the drugs have made me that stupid?"

"There's no need to raise your voice; the nurse is watching you."

"Well, don't tell me a pack of lies then."

"My father is in London. He drove down to Pembroke to see me."

"Rubbish, why didn't Allan or Amina tell me that?"

"Because they didn't know, Emre must keep it a secret. He has claimed asylum here."

"So nobody knows but you. That's very convenient."

"It's not convenient; nobody must know; remember, they don't know Emre is my father."

"How is George?"

"Fine, as far as I know."

"You must think I am a fool. If Emre was here, which is impossible, he would have demanded that he saw me."

"Ali, you're getting worked up over nothing. I was with my father."

"Lies, you were with George."

"Ali, what's this all about."

"I know George."

"You know me better. Are you accusing me of being unfaithful?"

"Look at me; take a bloody good look. Who could blame you?"

"Ali, I would never be unfaithful." *Can he read the lie?* "So please don't hurt me; stop accusing me."

"Okay, where were you then?"

"I was with my father, we went to Barafundle Bay, it was lovely, he wants to visit you. Do you want to see him? Are you ready for that?"

"Are you hoping the drugs will kick in and I won't remember this conversation tomorrow?"

"I hope you remember it well and apologise for your accusations; what is wrong with you?"

Ali screamed, "Everything, every fucking thing!"

The screams went straight to the pit of my stomach, and his body tensed as though he was fitting. Nurses rushed to his bed, one with a needle and two with extra pillows. I was told to go, as they pushed me out of the way. The nurses pulled up the bedside rails and placed the pillows against Ali's body.

"What's happening? Please tell me."

One of the nurses said, "Please go now; you are in the way."

Another nurse said, "He's fitting, having a grand mal seizure."

The nurses must have paged Doctor Phillips; he appeared rushing towards me as I walked down the corridor.

He looked at his pager as he ran past me and curtly said, panting, "Later, my office, please."

I waited a few minutes in his office before he returned and sat opposite me, looking a little flustered and said, "Sorry, it's been one of those days."

"I have never seen Ali like this; what's happened?"

"He's had a fit; it's under control. Did you say anything to upset him?"

"Not really; he got agitated over something."

"When you were last here, I told you about CBT."

"Yes, I remember. Cognitive behavioural therapy, right?"

"Yes, we expected Ali to react negatively to the treatment; initially, it's normal. Each person responds differently. According to what he's experienced, his personality or brain damage, finding out these things is always a balancing act."

"Oh, so what have you found out?"

"Quite a lot. I am not going into detail, but Ali was brutally tortured. He is a strong-willed man. I think he will come to terms with the torture, the physical damage, except for what they did to his reproductive organs."

"So he remembers everything now?"

"No, I don't think so; more to come slowly."

"Ali behaved like he hated me. Why would he do that?"

"Well, you need to talk to a behavioural therapist. I can arrange that, and they will talk you through it; it's not unusual."

"Would it be okay to talk to my friend, the psychiatrist?"

"You could, but he didn't witness Ali's reaction. We have experts here, you understand, so I think it's better not to."

"You mentioned mental issues. What do you mean?"

"Besides everything else they did to him, his skull is damaged, evidence of being repeatedly beaten, which could cause psychological brain damage."

"What does that mean?"

"Well, you have heard about concussions caused by repeated bangs to the head; depending on what part of the brain was damaged, it affects people in different ways."

"How can you tell if his brain is damaged?"

"Today, we are lucky. We have the technology to discover which part of his brain has been damaged and which thought patterns, emotions, etcetera."

"When will the tests be done?"

"After today's seizure, we'll bring it forward in the next couple of days."

"So his sense of reasoning might be damaged?"

"We will find out after the scans have been done and analysed; you will be told then the prognosis and treatment." Looking at the door, the doctor said, "So, if you don't mind, it's been a hell of a day."

That evening, I phoned George. "I need to talk to someone. Are you alone?"

"No... Well, if you are quick, Hua is in the kitchen.

Nothing personal, if you know what I mean," George whispered.

"No, of course not. I saw Ali today. I told him where I had been, and he didn't believe me."

"That doesn't sound like Ali. Where did he think you were?"

"Sorry, George, with you."

He whispered again, "Have you told him anything about the other night?"

"Only that we met and how you had changed and settled down, nothing else."

"Okay, what did his doctors say? You did ask, yes?"

"They think he may have suffered some concussions. He had a seizure today."

"How bad was it?"

"Bloody awful, they called it a grand mal."

"Not nice to witness."

"No, it wasn't, and he may have brain damage."

Oh, I see; they might suspect a personality disorder then."

"Yes, George, they said as much."

In the background, I heard, "Who are you talking to, George?"

"Hua's just walked in. Do you want to say hi to Margaret?"

"Hi Hua, I've heard so much about you. We must meet sometime."

"Yes, we must… I'll pass you back to George."

"I've been thinking, has Ali been told the extent of his injuries?"

I whispered, "Hua was rather abrupt."

"Don't worry, she's busy, that's all."

"Apologise for me for interrupting her."

"No problem, I will."

"Where were we? Yes, there are more tests."

"Okay, I shouldn't say this. I am not Ali's doctor, but he might be pushing you away because he thinks it's unfair on you."

"George, that's ridiculous. Ali wouldn't do that."

"You did it to him, remember?"

"George, that's not the same thing."

"What, you mean feeling incomplete, not feeling a real woman, lying to Ali? I could go on."

"Ali wouldn't do that to me; he just wouldn't."

"Maybe the old Ali wouldn't have, but…"

Hua spoke close to the phone, "George, stop there; you have said enough to Margaret. Pass me the phone."

"Margaret, George isn't always right. Listen to what your doctors tell you," Hua said confidently, adding, "I've just put the speaker on."

George butted in, "No, you don't have to listen to me but remember how Ali had to fight for you. You may have to do the same. That's all."

I could hear Hua in the background mumbling, "Leave it, George, for God's sake."

"Okay, George, Hua, I'll keep an open mind and do my best."

George replied, "Okay, let me know how it goes."

Hua mumbled again, "Jesus, George, let go."

"Thanks for your help, both."

"Keep in touch," George said. I could hear Hua mumbling but couldn't catch what she said.

The following day, Doctor Phillips phoned to ask me to stay away for a few days. My father wanted me to join him at his apartment whenever I was free, so I rang him, but he didn't seem happy – distant as though not really listening, so I asked, "Is there anything wrong?"

He replied curtly, "Wait till you get here."

Soon after I arrived, I did that directly after our usual hug. But the hug was subdued and shorter this time, not his customary 'doesn't-want-to-let-go hug'. I asked, "What's up, Baba?"

"Please sit. I have heard disturbing news from Syria."

"Not more bad news, Baba."

"I've heard that the government is rounding up high-ranking dissidents."

"It was bound to happen. Forced into doing the government's dirty work while knowing it was wrong was bound to breed dissidents."

"All of us knew but were scared, so we just went along because of what the alternative was."

"So, what's changed? You already knew this when you got out."

"Fatima phones regularly to check I am okay. I get the latest news then."

"Do you both feel something for each other still?"

"I told you I loved her dearly once, but that's not why she phones. She always has questions about you. In her own mind, she still really thinks of you as her daughter."

"Okay, but what has upset you?"

"When the calls stopped, it seemed strange."

"When was that?"

"A short time ago, maybe a few weeks."

"So, you're worried she is one of those arrested as dissidents?"

"Yes, extremely so, or something has happened to her."

"But she was pro-government, wasn't she part of the secret service?"

"Yes, she was, but she never told me anything about her work. I never knew what she thought. When I asked many years ago, she said best you don't know."

"Do you think she turned against the government then?"

"I don't know if she did, but I know she somehow got me out with genuine papers."

"You think they found out what she did?"

"I don't know, maybe?"

"Maybe she got others out as well; perhaps she used her position to do good?"

"She told me I was being watched and to get out quickly."

"So you think she was suspected of getting you out?"

"I don't know, maybe everyone was being watched, so I suppose so."

"Did you know you were being spied on before Fatima told you?"

"Not, really; if something seemed odd, I said nothing. Frightened to speak, who could I confide in?"

"You didn't do anything wrong, did you?"

"Other than turning a blind eye to what was going on for years, complicit, you could say. I am ashamed I wasn't brave enough to act."

"If you had stayed, you would have to be one of them or a dissident?"

"Yes, so I fled like a coward."

"You were ushered out safely by Fatima; I wouldn't call that being a coward. I wish Ali had done the same and insisted we escaped when we could have, but he was brave. Look at us now."

"I don't know who to contact to find out where she is. I still have ex-colleagues, but knowing who to trust is the problem. I have been racking my brains and drawn a blank."

"Sorry, Baba, I can't be of any help there. I don't know of any of her friends."

After cooking a meal between us, we sat close to each other on the sofa. The television was on. Neither of us was engrossed in anything. I asked myself, *who does Fatima know that I do? No one.* And then I had an out-of-the-blue brainwave. *Yes, there is one person we both know and have spoken to.* Before speaking, I pondered for a while before asking my father, "Do you know if Fatima has left a will?"

"No, I don't; why do you ask?"

"Because you insist that Fatima treats me like I am her daughter, yes? So, do you think she may have left a will in my favour?"

"Knowing her, yes, but what's the point? We are not in Syria."

"Do you know if she had a solicitor?"

"No, where are you going with this? I still don't get the point."

"Have you heard of a Mr Morris?"

"Remind me."

"He's the solicitor Fatima used to keep track of me."

"Ah, yes, now I can see where you are going, clever girl."

"Well, do you think they could still be in contact?"

"For what reason?"

"Maybe she's been in contact with him regarding her will, me being her make-believe daughter."

"She has no one other than me or you, so maybe it's worth a punt."

"Do you think she might still be in contact with Mr Morris?"

"Maybe."

"Tomorrow, you should call Mr Morris. It's worth a try."

Chapter 18

The Letters

I phoned Mr Morris's office at nine o'clock the following morning, impatient for answers.

"Morris's Solicitors, can I help you?"

"Can I speak to Mr Morris, please?"

After a slight pause, the secretary answered, "Sorry, Mr. Morris died a few years back."

"Oh, sorry to hear that. He was a lovely man. Who has taken over his caseload?"

"Can I ask who's calling?"

"Sorry, I should have said it's Margaret Mansour."

"Hang on, I'll find out who oversees your file and transfer you. It won't take a moment..."

"Hello, I'm Brian Hurst. How can I help?"

"On the off-chance, I wonder if you have anything for me."

"Well, yes, I have letters for you and one for Emre Hamoud. From Fatima Hamoud. You can collect them anytime."

"Why haven't you contacted me?" As I asked the question, I realised it was stupid. The only address they had for me was in Syria. "Sorry, there's no need to answer.

How could you have? When can we come in to collect them?"

"Anytime."

"Today, this afternoon?"

"Fine, see you then, after two o'clock, okay?

"See you then."

Emre overheard the conversation, and he looked pleased. I assumed it was because Fatima was still in contact, so maybe she was safe. "One thing about Fatima you can rely on is proper diligence." With a smile, he added, "Perhaps we should make the day of it and have lunch out; what do you think?"

"That would be lovely. Keep my mind off what's in the letters."

After lunch, we went to the solicitor's office and were shown into Mr Morris's old, musty office; nothing had changed much. Still, a typical solicitors office stuck in a Victorian time warp. In Mr Morris's antique leather chair sat his replacement. Weird, such a young man seemed out of place in the setting. He held his hand for me to shake. I recalled what Ali always said: if you are going to shake a hand, grip it firmly, not hard, but enough so that it's felt. So I did that; my grip wasn't strong, so I gave it my best, looking Mr Hurst in the eye as I did. I don't know who felt more embarrassed as his hand crumpled in my grip and his young cheeks flushed. Emre gave the same manly handshake, smiling at me as he realised what had happened.

"Right, let's get down to business. I have two letters, one for each of you; they came a few weeks ago." I could see the letters on the table clearly addressed to us. "Before handing them to you, I have a question. I have been instructed by Fatima Hamoud to ask a question, a sort of password, if you like. Is there a place in Pembrokeshire with special memories for both of you?"

We both said, "Yes." We looked at each other, puzzled.

"Well, what is it?" he said with an air of authority.

We both said, "Barafundle Bay." Young Mr Hurst slid the letters to both of us.

Emre looked at the front closely, not opening it and said, "Fatima's handwriting."

I opened my letter first. Father and Mr. Hurst were waiting for my reaction. The envelope contained a letter and a photo. The photo had been taken from a distance, so I had to look closely. I first recognised the stone arch leading to the steep steps down onto Barafundle Beach. *Strange, why?* Then, I looked closely at the two figures standing under the arch. A man and a woman. "Shit, sorry, how could this happen?" It was my father and me, holding hands; I remember standing with him, admiring the beautiful view.

By this time, my father had opened his envelope, and he, too, had a photograph and a letter. I looked at him, and he looked back at me with watery eyes, uttering, "How the blazes?"

I passed my photo to him, and he held them together for comparison; I could see the emotion welling on his face as he passed them to me. One shot was a lot older but was taken at the exact location. The photo was of a man and a woman looking at the same view. I looked closer and realised it was a photo of my mother and father. My father asked Mr Hurst, "Is it okay to read the letters privately?"

"No problem with that at all. Giving you the letters was all I was contracted to do."

Sitting in the car before setting off, I asked my father, "What do the photos mean?"

"Looks like Fatima is up to her old spying tricks again."

"But why?"

"I don't know; the letters might be a clue. Let's wait until we get home before reading them."

"Yes, okay with me."

Father said, "First, let's sit and relax before diving into the letters; they are addressed privately, so maybe that's what we do."

"If you say so, but I have no secrets from you, Baba."

So we sat in a different corner of the room. My father waited for me to take my letter out of my envelope before he did the same.

Dear Margaret

I know you will never forgive me. I see you as my child; I watched you grow into a wonderful young woman. I hope you will one day thank me for my little part. I know you are now where you always wanted to be with your father. All the paperwork Mr Morris held for me is yours if you want it.

He also has a will that he will open. It's not a lot, but it will help.

You are reading this letter now because I instructed Mr Hurst to give it to you if he hadn't heard from me within an allotted time.

I hope Ali recovers.

With all my love always.
Fatima Hamoud xx
Ps. Please beware of Professor George Newall.

"Baba, do you think Fatima is alive?"

"Sorry Margaret, I haven't finished reading the letter yet. Give me a minute or two to digest it."

I waited patiently for my father to finish reading his letter. I read mine several times over and compared the two photos.

"Well, Margaret, it will take some time to sink in. I will tell you what you need to know."

"Okay, Baba, shall I read my letter out loud in full first?"

My father nodded in approval. I omitted the warning about George, though still puzzled as to why Fatima should have warned me. *What does she know?*

"Right, Margaret, now my letter is much like yours, except she explains about the photos. Every person on our delegation who visited Pembrokeshire all those years ago was monitored, as you know. The photo taken then was one of many; Fatima destroyed most of them because they were of a very personal nature."

"That's a shame; I understand why and would have been jealous and done the same."

"Let me continue. When Fatima did her magic and got me safely to England, there was a risk that I would be discovered by loyal Syrian activists living in the UK. So, she arranged surveillance to keep an eye on me. Travelling from London to Pembroke was a trigger for me being observed closely. The photo of you and me taken at Barafundle Bay was to confirm it was me and that you were not a threat."

"How could Fatima arrange surveillance here? Is she in touch with the secret service, MI5?"

"No, she explains a little in the letter. There's is a phone number to call and a password to confirm who I am. I can't tell you until I have rung the number."

"Do you know who you are calling?"

"Well, I suppose you can know this; it's Amnesty International."

"I have heard of them; what do they do?"

"I am not entirely sure, but I know they do a lot of work globally helping people. I have heard nothing bad."

"Are you going to call them now?"

"Let me think a while. What question to ask? Has something happened to Fatima? I will sleep on it and try and figure it out."

Giggling, I said, "You are sure I am your daughter? I would have been on the phone now."

Smiling, he replied, "You take after your mother, very impatient."

"I would have said controlling, in a nice way."

Baba said, "Okay, let's think of something else before we go to bed." And he turned the BBC 10 o'clock news on, as he always did.

The following morning, I heard my father rattling around in the kitchen. *Why does making a cup of tea sound like an alarm call? Maybe it was intended to be?* I stayed in bed, hoping a cup of tea would appear next to me, and pretended to be asleep, like most mornings. The tea didn't arrive, so I was curious. I listened as my father talked on the phone as I quietly opened my door.

"I have been given this number to call… Fatima Hamoud…" I couldn't hear what my father said next. Then his voice got a little louder. "Carol Fraser."

What? Why has my mother's name been involved in this? Ah, password? Of course, using a dead person's name is clever but still unnerving. I decided to cover my ears with a pillow so as not to pry but ask my father later what was said. I nodded off to sleep again. I often did that lately, almost fully awake, deciding to get up in a few minutes, then discovered the clock had gained an hour.

Father stood by the boiling kettle when I entered the kitchen, and toast popped up in the toaster. "I heard you in the shower; I didn't disturb you earlier. I thought you needed a lie-in."

"That's okay. I did need it. Did I hear you on the phone earlier?"

"Yes, after breakfast, we'll chat, okay?"

"Lovely, can't wait to hear what you've learned."

"Marmalade or blackcurrant jam?"

"Either, Baba, surprise me."

After our second cup of tea – I proved I could be patient – I said, "Well, what did whoever say on the phone?"

"Fatima has been supplying Amnesty International with information regarding Sednaya Prison in Damascus."

I had heard of it and the rumours of what was happening there. "I see."

"Fatima had proof gained from escaped ex-guards."

"Escaped? Why would they escape?"

"Because of what they were forced to do."

"I have heard rumours, horrible things. Are they true?"

"Apparently so; Fatima passed what evidence she had onto Amnesty International, which will be used by the international criminal courts eventually."

"I was told by a nurse in Antalya about the prison. The popular name for Sedanya prison is the 'human slaughterhouse. Thousands are being executed."

"That's awful; what had these people done?"

"Nothing, people like you. That's what Fatima saved you from."

"I heard rumours but didn't want to believe them."

"So, where is Fatima? Is she safe? I can see by your face you think the worst."

"They don't know but will let me know if they find anything out."

Chapter 19

Hua

The phone rang. Half asleep, I looked at the clock: seven thirty-something. *Who rings now?* Nervous. *Has something happened to Ali? Please, no more shocking news.*

"Hello… Anyone there?"

"It's Hua. Can we talk?"

The squawky Asian tone of her voice unnerved me. *Bloody hell, what does she want this time in the morning?*

"What about?"

"What do you think? George, of course."

"What about George?"

"Margaret, don't act stupid with me."

"Sorry, you must explain. I am not stupid; I just woke up."

"You've slept with George, haven't you? Don't lie."

"Not really." *That sounds stupid.*

"You either have or have not, which is it?"

"I needed a shoulder to cry on; George was there for me. It isn't what you think."

"How do you know what I think?"

"Sorry, if anything happened, it wasn't Georges' fault; it was mine."

"So you shagged George, which had nothing to do with him."

"It wasn't like that; he helped me."

"Margaret, you are a fool; George helped himself."

"No, Hua, he has changed. He told me all about you and how you changed him."

"I finished with George last night; you're not the first. He's a serial shagger, but you know that."

"Did George explain what happened?"

"No, he didn't need to. He told me he went to visit a male friend in hospital. I rang the ward, and the nurse looking after his friend told me he hadn't seen him."

"Do you constantly check up on him?"

"Only since he promised he wouldn't do it again."

"It?"

"Shag anything on two legs."

"Has he done it before?"

"He promised the last one was his last. He swore on it."

"It was my fault. I needed someone."

"George used you. He is very clever. He made you think he was doing you a favour."

"How do you know that?"

"I rang the hotel where he was staying, and the receptionist asked who was calling. I told her I was his secretary, and she told me he had just come in with his wife. She said he was a charming man; he insisted on a double bed when booking in and said his wife would join him later."

"But he didn't know I would ask him if I could stay the night."

"If it hadn't been you, it would have been someone else."

"Hua, I think you have got him all wrong; he's changed."

"Leopard, spots, say no more."

"I think you are wrong, Hua; people can change, George has."

"Whatever."

"Sorry, Hua, I didn't mean to hurt anyone."

"Me too. Bye, Margaret."

"Who was that on the phone?" Father shouted from the kitchen.

"Just a friend of a friend." I was glad my father couldn't see my face.

"That's nice, teas up."

"Okay, in a minute."

After breakfast, prepared by my father again, I apologetically announced, "My turn next."

Father gave me that 'when I see it, I will believe it' look. Then he asked, "I would love to see Ali. Can you check if we can visit soon?"

"Let's just go without asking; I would love to see the expression of surprise on Ali's face." I hoped that would be all that he would see.

"You sure he can cope with both of us?"

"Baba, he would love to see you." *I felt guilty. Was I trying to prove to Ali my alibi?*

So that's what we did: turn up unexpectedly and ask to visit Ali. The ward sister agreed it would be all right, but his reaction would determine how much time we could spend with him. On the journey to the hospital, I told my father, "Try not to show pity; treat him as you always have."

"I won't be shocked, promise; I already have a picture in my head."

Ali was sitting in bed, looking bored; maybe he wasn't expecting any visitors. I walked into his room first, with Emre a little behind as a surprise. As usual, I walked to the side of his bed, which blocked Ali's view of the doorway. Ali seemed a little unsure. *Possibly remembering his previous outburst.* When I stepped to the side, Emre came into Ali's view. Ali couldn't comprehend what was happening until Emre embraced him and kissed him on both cheeks, hugging him tightly as good Arab friends do.

Emre said earnestly, "You look like you are on the mend."

"Getting better slowly," Ali said whilst smiling at me.

That smile meant so much; I had waited so long to see it, and he did look better. *I don't know what they are doing to him, but it's working.*

Ali asked Emre, "Did Fatima get out, too? Where are you living?"

Emre shook his head to the first question and replied, "London."

Ali looked a little bemused but didn't press Emre. I showed Ali the photo of me taken at Barafundle Bay with Emre, and Emre showed the picture of Emre with my mother. Ali looked at me sheepishly and said, "Maybe one day, we three could go there together; maybe Fatima could join us."

"Imagine that, Baba."

Father didn't reply but managed a smile he used when unsure.

I told Ali about old doddery Mr Morris dying. Ali replied, "He was a kind old man. If he hadn't turned a blind eye, we would have never found your father."

Emre left so we could spend a little time together. I was so pleased that Ali had smiled at me. I hugged him again and whispered in his ear, "I love you."

"Love you too; I am sorry for accusing you of lying."

"That's all right; you weren't thinking straight."

"You weren't here; George was supposed to be. My head wasn't in a good place, so, as the saying goes, I put two and two together."

"How did you know George was supposed to be here?"

"His partner rang, asking to speak to him; he wasn't here. So, the nurse was expecting him to turn up. She told me he was coming and asked if I wanted to see him."

"What did you say?"

"I said yes, though I was glad he didn't come. I didn't want him to see me like this, but he had come a long way."

"He didn't turn up then." *I'm digging a deeper hole for myself.*

"Nor you, but I know now you were with Emre. Sorry again."

"No need, darling; in a way, I am glad I stayed away. You look so much better; what's happening regarding your treatment?" *I didn't feel guilty. In my head, I made love to Ali, not George.*

"What haven't they tried? Everything seems to help; now, they are trying out EDMR."

"What does that stand for?"

"Eye movement desensitisation and reprocessing. It's all to do with following a light whilst talking about the bad things that happened."

"And does that help?"

"I think it might. It's hard to tell. I am also reluctantly doing group therapy."

"How are you getting on with that?"

"I thought it wasn't for me. I thought learning about others' issues would make it worse."

"Did it? I can't imagine you talking to anyone about personal things; you're such a private person."

"Me too, but it's a bit like when you are part of a team in the army; you all muck in to help each other."

"Like bonding?"

"Yes, exactly like that. We understand and lean on each other, realising what the others have gone through somehow lessens my load."

"Like you used to say, knowing someone has got my back is reassuring."

"Yes, exactly; ask George about it next time you see him."

"Yes, I will." *Oh no, what a web.*

"Thinking about George, I'm ready to see him now; it's been a long time. Can you let him know?"

"He's very busy, so I can't promise."

"I'm not going anywhere for a while, so there's no rush."

"Okay, I'll give him a ring soon, promise." I kissed Ali again and said goodbye. On the way out, I asked the ward sister, "How's he doing?"

"Very well. If you imagine a graph, he's halfway up the slope. When he hits the cusp, things get tricky as he must negotiate the downward slope to normality, free fall if you like, without brakes. That can be a rough ride for both of you; he will need you more than ever."

"But he is getting better. I can see it, isn't he?"

"Yes, he is. We nurse him up the slope, but there's a long way to go. The next step will be to get him out of here for a change, a sort of holiday. Could you cope with that?"

"I hope so. I have some friends longing to help. Would it be possible to stay with them?"

"Do you mean George and his wife?"

"No, not them. She's a partner, not wife anyway." *Why did I need to correct her?*

"Whoever it is, we would like to vet them. Is that okay?"

"I'll ask them, but I know their answer. In fact, I'll ask them tonight."

"Good, see you tomorrow."

Father was waiting patiently, with that smile of approval, which made me feel warm inside; we walked to the car, arms locked together.

Raising my spirits, he said, "He looks better than I imagined." He squeezed my arm a little.

"Better than the last time I saw him. The sister has asked if I can arrange for Ali to spend time in the real world."

"He can stay with us."

"Baba, I think they meant somewhere he could be outside, in the fresh air in the countryside. I was thinking of taking him to see Allan and Amina. That would mean leaving you on your own. Unless, of course, we tell them who you really are, and you come too."

"I don't think it's wise for them to know. There is a saying about idle tongues."

"They're not like that. They would never tell anyone."

"I can't take the risk until I know Fatima is safe."

"Probably be for the best. It would be hard to explain why you have always been a secret anyway."

I phoned Amina and asked if it would be possible for Ali and me to join them for a short holiday. They were delighted. So, I called the ward sister to tell her I had started the ball rolling and asked what was next. After telling her it was Pembrokeshire, her tone changed, and she sounded a little concerned and asked, "Could they come here so I can talk to them?"

Perplexed, I asked, "Why? It's a long way to come for an interview."

"Exactly, it's a long way away. That's why we need to see if they are suitable."

"Of course they are; they are our closest friends."

"That's not what the screening will be about; there are other things, like do they realise how ill Ali is, is their property suitable, etcetera."

"Well, the answers are yes, yes, and yes to anything else. I wouldn't have asked them if I didn't think they were suitable."

I could hear the irritation in the sister's voice as she replied, "Unfortunately, the decision is not up to you."

Allan and Amina agreed to attend the interview the following week. When they arrived at Frimley, they met Ali in the day room after being told by the sister not to show too much emotion. The sister and I watched as they approached Ali, sitting in a bay window. Sunbeams lit up the area. When Ali saw them enter, he smiled like he always did. His new dentures, not fully bedded in, looked too large for his gaunt face. Allan managed to restrain himself, but Amina couldn't; she flung herself into Ali's arms. The sister gave me a knowing glance.

I shrugged my shoulders and smiled back. All three stood together in the sunbeam, embracing like an end scene from a Disney movie. They appeared to be talking excitedly, possibly about the upcoming visit and seeing the kids again.

The sister precisely timed how long the visit would last. Then she appeared in the doorway with an air of authority, announcing, "Visiting time is over."

While I sat with Ali, the sister interviewed Allan and Amina in her office. Later, they told me there were things they had to do to their property before he would be allowed to stay there. They would be guided by a local social worker who would inspect their house and offer guidance and help. Armed with guidance leaflets, Allan and Amina waved goodbye, promising they would do all they could as swiftly as possible.

After they left, the sister called me into her office for a chat. "They both seem lovely. They listened to all I said, though what impressed me was they both listened earnestly to every word."

"Yes, that's them; that's what they are like. I knew you would like them."

"Can we move on? You must always be there if Ali is approved to stay with your friends. Are you okay with that?"

"Of course. Where else would I be?"

"You have other close friends, I believe?"

"What has that got to do with anything?"

"Nothing, but Ali always comes first. Are you sure you can manage that?"

"Are you thinking about the other week when I visited friends?"

"Well, yes, you weren't here when Ali needed you, and when you did visit, he had a seizure."

"It wasn't my idea to stay away. It was Dr. Phillips." *Does she know differently?*

The sister gave me a knowing look. "Okay, if you say so. You will be his primary carer if Ali can stay with your friends. Are you okay with that?"

"Yes."

"Well, you will have to have training. I will set that up with his lead nurse. You okay to start learning?"

"Yes!"

The sister looked startled at my quick response and asked sharply, "When?"

"Now." *Two can play that game.*

"Okay, I'll set up a training session; when the nurse and the social worker in Pembrokeshire are satisfied, we can think about the visit."

"Fine."

"Mrs Mansour, have I rattled your cage?"

"No."

"Have it your way."

The training involved the everyday things anyone would do nursing a sick patient at home. The additional training precisely recorded his medication in a special booklet, as the nurse insisted. I had to administer and witness Ali taking his medication and then record it in a book at the exact time. I had to monitor and record his blood pressure, temperature and heart rate. I had to note mood swings in another book and anything that seemed odd or affected him. When the lead nurse approved my work, we signed my acceptance form. I was given the emergency phone number at Frimley. I was given the local district nurse's and social worker's phone numbers. They would check on Ali weekly and were on call if I needed assistance. Ali enjoyed the extra attention from me, as I took a lot more time doing things, so he had my company for a longer time. It made me feel I was doing something worthwhile.

A date was set for the Pembroke visit in a couple of weeks. I couldn't wait. I couldn't imagine how much Ali looked forward to escaping being locked up. In one way or another, he hadn't spent much time outside except for the occasional walk around the garden at Frimley. I wondered if he would be excited, apprehensive, or a mixture of both. At least it would be something different. I was nervous as his prime carer and excited that Ali was finally getting better.

Ali asked, "Have you asked George if he is coming to visit? I'd love to see him before we go away."

"Tonight, I'll give him a call. I can't promise; as I said, he's a remarkably busy man."

"Why don't you ask him to bring his girlfriend as well? I'd love to see her, the one that managed to capture him. She must be something special."

Oh shit!

Reluctantly I phoned George to tell him that Ali wanted to see him. "I would love to. Tell me when; I can't wait."

"Don't you feel guilty about the other night?"

"Hell no, helping a friend in need, why should I?"

"I think you should know; Hua doesn't see it your way."

"So she contacted you? What a selfish cow."

"George, come on now, you told me she was the one."

"Jesus, I tried, but she is too bloody jealous."

"She has a point, George. Didn't you explain it wasn't like she thought?"

"I tried, but she would never understand."

"So, you have moved on then?"

"No, not yet."

"But you will?"

"Bears, shit, forest, maybe another shot at Hua."

"Okay, George, tread carefully. You might stand in something the bear left behind."

"Margaret, are you free for dinner one night?"

"You're incorrigible. Yes, just dinner would be fine."

George visited Ali without me; my excuse to myself was that they would have more time together. The real reason was I didn't feel confident that what happened between George and me wouldn't show. So, I arranged for George to collect me from the Travelodge after visiting time.

George collected me with a formal smile and a pat on the back as I got into his car. After a few drinks, I told George about Ali's recovery plan; he probably knew, as he was still talking to Dr. Phillips.

Then, I started the conversation about the elephant in the room. "George, I am so sorry you and Hua have broken up. It was all my fault."

"No need, I am a grown man; I knew what I was doing. In my eyes, I wasn't being unfaithful."

"But Hua told me you'd done it before."

"Yeah, once before, but I promised her never again, and I meant it."

"George, you are playing with me. You can't help yourself, can you?"

"No, not when it's helping a friend."

"George, you're good, too bloody good." The few glasses of wine loosened my tongue. "George, it would never have happened if things had been different."

"I don't think you should talk too much under the influence of alcohol."

I deliberately took another large swig of the red wine. I swished it around my mouth like a connoisseur, giving me extra time to think. "George, I need to talk. I haven't told anyone properly what happened to me."

"Is this the right place to talk, Margaret? It's not just me that can hear every word."

Raising my voice, I replied, "Very clever, George. Are you asking me back to your place for a nightcap?"

"Shush, if you want, but just to listen, that's all."

"You're so good, so bloody good."

George placed his index finger on his lips, gave me a look so I understood, called the waiter, settled the bill, and apologised to the waiter for the noise.

George man-handled tipsy me into the front seat of his sports car and said, "Where to?"

"You are the perfect gentleman, George, somewhere dark, very dark."

"Are you sure, this is a sportscar?"

"Don't get ahead of yourself, George. Just drive."

George pulled into a quiet lane, found a spot hidden from the road and switched off the lights. The night air somehow made me feel lightheaded; the effect of the bottle of red wine consumed took more effect. "George, can you sit there and listen? Please don't butt in until I have finished." *Was he anticipating something else?*

"Okay, get it off your chest."

"I have never spoken to anyone else about what I will tell you. I told you the other night I was raped in Aleppo."

"Hmm, yes."

"The word rape indicates that the sex was carried out without consent. There is no single word that describes what was done to me. It wasn't a man entering me without my permission. It was about degradation, pain, hate, sneering, loathing, filthy bodies, kicking, and hitting because I was a woman. The pleasure they took wasn't sexual; it was evil, there are no words to describe what they did to me, but it was not rape. That single word doesn't cover it. Afterwards, when the doctor helped me clean myself, I still felt dirty; the word dirty doesn't cover it. There is no way I could get you to understand what I felt. Afterwards, I scrubbed myself till I bled, and I haven't felt clean since then. The smell of the creatures that did this to me is with me forever. It wasn't just my body they violated; they did something to my mind."

I felt George's comforting hand on my knee. "I don't know what to say."

"Sorry, George, I didn't mean to upset you, but I haven't finished yet. When Ali came home after the rape, I didn't want him to touch me. For a while, we hadn't made love. What Ali had seen affected him; we didn't talk about it. Perhaps he couldn't. We didn't sleep like spoons after the rape because it didn't feel the same to me. Instead of two perfect spoons cast in the same mould, we were like odd wooden spoons that didn't belong together. When I cuddled you the other night, I imagined you were Ali, and we felt like a perfect set of spoons again. Can you understand or explain that?"

"Margaret, I am not your therapist, but I think you still love Ali and want his love."

"But what if my Ali doesn't return? Instead, someone that this awful world has created."

"It takes time; your Ali is still there; they will find him, hopefully."

I didn't mention that Ali would never fully return and that part of our relationship was lost forever. "Thanks for listening to my offloading. I needed it. Now, what about you and Hua?"

"Anytime you want to talk, I will always be here, you know? As far as Hua, it's up to her."

"Thanks, George, you're not such a prat."

"Fancy a nightcap?"

"Prat."

As George started the engine, I said, "George, when you were young, you dressed in a bohemian way because you realised that some girls liked that. As you got older, the young girls got older too. You then realise older women look for a successful man. So, you ditched your bohemian look and went for something suave. What comes next, George? Can't you just be you? I bet you don't even own a pair of jeans now, do you?

"I never looked at it like that; I thought I was just growing up, adapting."

"George, you have never grown up; you are still the kid in the candy store."

"Is that a dreadful thing? I am what I am, and there are several sweets I haven't tried yet. Perhaps denim on the older man will be the new look. I could then try a different shelf in the candy store."

"George, promise me the new jeans won't be ripped at the knees; you'd look a proper twat."

George followed my directions to my father's apartment. As he stopped the engine and switched off the lights, he observed, "Moved up in the world, then?"

"Not really, staying with family."

"Oh, I thought you didn't have any relations you knew of."

"I didn't think I had; Ali helped me trace him."

"Him?"

"Yes, a cousin."

"No chance of a nightcap, then?"

"Not the sort you like, George. Goodnight, George. Thanks for listening; you're not such a prat." George opened the passenger door to lift me out of the bucket seat. As he stood hugging me, I couldn't help saying, "You need to change your car. Remember, it's all about adapting. The ladies of your age prefer something a little more comfortable."

George said, "I think you're right; it's time to move on in many ways."

"Night. I'll ring you to let you know the visiting time, bye George and thanks again."

George visited Ali on his own several times; on one of these occasions, I phoned Hua, unsure if my call would be welcome. So, apprehensively, I asked, "Do you want to talk?"

She sounded obstructive and snapped," What about?"

"George, of course."

"You can have him."

"I don't want him."

"That makes two of us."

"He doesn't want me, don't be silly."

"You still slept with him, though, didn't you?"

"Hua, please, it's the same conversation we had last time; it wasn't like that. I have been George's friend for years."

"What about the others?"

"George told me that he made one mistake at the start of your relationship."

"You have been talking to George again; he put you up to this, didn't he."

"Yes, I have, and no, he doesn't know I am talking to you. He wants you back. I know that much." *I shouldn't have said that. George will be livid. Why did I get myself involved?*

"George doesn't know himself what he wants, so how do you know, you bloody psychic or something?"

"So, it's over for good then?"

"Thankfully, he's all yours now; that's what this call is about, right?

"No, it's not; you can't say I didn't try. Goodbye, Hua."

Chapter 20

Pembrokeshire

Allan and Amina collected us from Frimley Hospital and drove us to their home in Pembroke. When we loaded ourselves into the car, I realised how frail Ali seemed once outside the hospital. It may have been anxiety on his part, compounded by my own trepidation that we were doing the right thing. I also noticed that Allan and Amina were a little nervous and unsure how to act. So, the journey started in silence. Ali sat in the front, sitting next to Allan, who seemed to be driving more carefully than usual. Amina and I are in the back. In the old days, we chatted, ribbed each other, and told funny jokes or stories. Instead, it was an uneasy silence, all of us waiting for the other to speak.

Then Ali spoke, "I forgot how green England is." He always used to be the first to speak.

That was the signal for us slowly, one by one, adding, joining in, and saying the odd comment. But it was not like the banter of old. Hopefully, that would come later. Just straightforward talking, no ribbing each other, no laughing.

We arrived late and were greeted by Amara and Amal, who were obviously over-excited about meeting us after such a long time. Allan had warned them not to be too enthusiastic when welcoming Ali. In that respect, they took after their mother; they swarmed him with hugs and tears. Eventually, when it settled down again, Ali was first to speak. He expressed his surprise at how much they had grown, how beautiful Amara was, and how handsome Amal had become. *So far, so good.*

Going upstairs, I realised it had been a long time since I shared a bed with Ali. I must have understood this before, but somehow, the significance of it happening overwhelmed me. It did the same to Ali. He turned to face me. It was the first time I saw Ali cry because something good had happened for a long time.

After ensuring Ali's medication and everything else was recorded, we got into bed, faced each other, and switched the lights to dim. Ali wanted to talk and whispered, "Thank you for not giving up on me."

I whispered back, "Thank you for being you."

Ali's trembling woke me; his body felt stiff and wooden when I shook him to bring him out of what was happening. The crying and wailing started. I was instructed on what to do: slowly increase his medication. So, I whispered everything was okay and started to prepare his medication. Ali was now out of bed, curled up in the corner of the room, whimpering; it took all my strength to wrench his head into a position to give him the tablets and water. After a while, he slowly relaxed enough for me to coax him back into bed.

In the morning, I rang Dr. Phillips to confirm what I had done, more to assure myself than anything else. The doctor confirmed that I had done the right thing and asked if anything could have triggered him. I told him nothing had happened that day, except he met his godchildren for the first time in many years. Dr. Phillips concluded that the excitement might have been a little too much. I continued with the extra dose and reduced it if I noticed an adverse change in him.

We all drove to Freshwater East Beach the following day as we decided it was the most accessible. We set off with six people in the car, packed lunches and all the other paraphernalia for a day on the beach. The car park was only a short walk from the beach. I knew it would be a test for Ali, walking only a short distance, but I knew he was always up for a challenge.

So we spent time together watching the tide ebb and flow while the kids ran around with bats and balls, releasing pent-up energy. I watched Ali fall asleep in his deckchair. He looked content and woke after a little while with a smile. I felt there was hope that the old Ali was still inside the person beside me. Allan and Amina weren't close, so I talked loudly over the noise of the sea and wind, "I'd love to take you to Barafundle Bay, but it's a long walk; maybe when you are well." *That was a stupid thing to say.* Realising my foolish remark, I tried to change the subject, "Look at the kids running around; how they've grown."

"Did it bring back memories of your mother?"

That didn't work. "Yes, it did; it also brought back sad memories; now I know the full story."

"Can we go there on our own?"

"It's quite a walk from the car park when you are fit." *Oh no, I hope that's not a trigger?* "Sorry, Ali, I didn't mean to say that."

"That's okay. One day, though."

I smiled and held his hand. "One day."

Ali asked, "Do you think it's time to tell Allan and Amina who Emre is?"

"I'd love to tell them, but he said not until Fatima is safe."

"Why, where is she?"

"We don't know; we haven't heard anything since she got Emre out."

"Oh, I see."

Changing the subject, I asked, "What did you and George talk about?"

"Memories mostly, the good old times, he called them."

"Ali, do you think he has changed much?"

"He dresses smarter now. There's a thing you might remember about George. He gave the impression he didn't care about studying or how he looked. But he studied hard when no girl was in his room, and his beatnik look was just an act."

"Now he's matured, and so have his tactics, all very calculated; nothing has changed." *I can vouch for that.*

"The odd thing is it was always a different girl."

"Either he wasn't particularly good at keeping partners, or the experience for them wasn't as good as anticipated, or he has an obsessive-compulsive disorder, so it had to be someone new every time. I wonder if he studied OCD? If so, does he recognise it in himself?"

"Who knows? What's his new girl like?"

"I've only talked on the phone to her. Not sure she's a keeper, though."

"George told me the other night she is definitely the one."

What is George up to? "I suppose he's running out of options; all the good ones are snapped up, married with kids."

"Do you think that would have stopped the old George? You told me more than once that he had the morals of a tomcat."

"I think he will always be a tomcat."

"Remember he called you the ice maiden?"

"That's enough talk about George. Look at the kids, how they've changed. It won't be long before they start their lives as adults."

Allan ran over, obviously out of breath; keeping up with teenagers running in the sand was demanding work. He declared, "I'm thirsty. Do you fancy a pint on the way home?"

Ali was the first to respond. "Love one."

"Only the one, though, Allan. I am not sure about his meds."

"He'll be fine," Allan said. *I could tell it was without thinking.*

The kids joined in, deliberately sounding parched. "Me too, me too."

So we sat outside in a pub garden, the evening sun dappling us through the trees. In a melancholy tone, Ali said, "This brings back so many good memories. How could anyone ever think having a beer with friends is evil."

"Yes, it's a zillion miles away from life in Aleppo." I wanted to suck my words back into my mouth as soon as I said them. *Ali doesn't need to remember.*

Ali raised his glass and said, "Cheers, everyone."

The increased medication definitely worked. Ali slept better that night, with only a few whimpers and tossing and turning. This stopped when I comforted him by whispering that it was okay and gently shaking him. But I noticed he was a little drowsier and often fell asleep during the day if his mind wasn't engaged in what was happening around him. I assumed this was a good thing.

As the days rolled by, Ali insisted we spend time alone together. Allan or Amina would drop us off somewhere we could easily access the coast. We sat on a beach or the dunes, just the two of us, not saying much, just listening to the sea, wind, and birds. It was therapy for both of us. I never asked what he was thinking, and he never asked me. I assumed neither of us was thinking of the recent past. I remembered our beginning together and how the naïve Ali became part of my life. I hoped that the healthy, mature, confident man he became later would soon return.

The days flew into weeks; it was all about Ali for the James family and me. I couldn't thank them enough for being there for both of us. Preparing for the journey back to Frimley, I could see a change in him; instead of just being a passenger, he wanted to help load up the car. He was disappointed when he realised that most things were beyond his capabilities. Knowing Ali's determination, I assumed he would soon be able to share the load. Amina told us we were welcome anytime, so arrangements were made for a return visit later in the year.

Allan asked, "Why not come for Christmas?" So that was penned in, and we had something to look forward to.

Chapter 21

Fatima

Emre regularly contacted Amnesty International, enquiring about the whereabouts of Fatima. He had so many questions that bothered him. He already knew she was responsible for his freedom, and he wondered if there were others she saved. He confided in me the guilt he felt was because Fatima risked her life to save him. His contact was always quite blunt, continuing to reply with the word 'classified' to most of his questions. There were so many people missing. Perhaps it was a way of not getting emotionally involved, or there were too many, or maybe he just didn't care. Whatever the reason, it added to Emre's frustration.

When Amina urgently needed a visa at the start of the war, Ali asked Emre to get one so the James family could flee war-torn Syria. Emre told me it was Fatima who organised everything, not himself. For Fatima's safety, Emre hadn't disclosed this to anyone until now. That planted a seed in his mind, and mine too, that it wasn't the first time she had helped others as it was done so efficiently. We both became concerned that maybe she worked undercover, assisting dissidents or anyone who needed to escape the country and had been doing so for some time.

Sometime later, his contact at Amnesty International phoned Emre with information regarding Fatima. He now had confirmation that she had been arrested, charged with treason, and signed a declaration that she was guilty.

Emre was distraught, raging at the agent, "Fatima would not do that. She would not sign anything she hadn't done."

The agent replied, "Yes, I know that. She is a significant loss to us, too."

"What do you mean by 'loss to us'?"

"I can tell you now; she helped investigate war crimes for us."

"What do you mean by 'loss to us'?"

"Sorry… I thought you realised that signing you are guilty means she is dead."

"She wouldn't sign a lie; she could still be alive."

"Mr Hamoud, sorry, I must be blunt. She is undoubtedly dead."

Through rage and tears, Emre screamed, "I don't believe you! How can you be so sure!"

"Because they arrested 100 dissidents the same day. They individually took them to a room to complete paperwork confirming their name, title, status, etc. It took about two minutes. When 30 or so people had signed the papers, they would have been told it was all a mistake. Then, they were escorted to another part of the prison for what they thought would be an apology and immediate release. They were then blindfolded, led into another room, and swiftly a noose was placed around their necks. The floor fell away. The process was over in seconds."

"How do you know this for sure?"

"We have defectors, escaped guards from the prison, who swear this is happening."

"So, Fatima signed her own death warrant without knowing. She wouldn't do that; she just wouldn't."

"Yes, I think she did; it was quick and matter-of-fact. Sign this piece of paper to prove who you are. There were no protests, trials or defence lawyers; people didn't realise what they were signing or were terrified to object."

"Do you have proof Fatima was definitely executed? How do you know for sure?"

"Proof? She was arrested on the same day we know others were executed."

"So, you are not sure then. There is a chance?"

"No, I don't think so."

"Is there a way of finding out for sure?"

"Not really. Just before the prisoners were hung, the guards fingerprinted everyone."

"Why do that?"

"The government's database can confirm the correct person has been executed."

"So that's the only way to tell for sure? Access to the database."

"Afraid so unless the database gets leaked."

"So, there is a chance of finding out then?"

"Not really. All the people that might leak information have been executed. Those left are aware of the consequences."

"What about your informants? Could they help?"

"Not really, they're only small fry. That's how they escaped. Witnessing what happened to traitors, they would be unlikely to risk their lives."

"Surely there must be a way?"

"We are working on it, but I am not confident. Sorry, but that's the truth."

Chapter 22

Christmas, 2015

I had anticipated that Ali's health would improve more rapidly than it did.

So, I was mindful that the Christmas trip to Pembroke would be a further test for Ali. Within the confines of Allan and Amina's home, Ali seemed to take most things in his stride. But he became agitated when confronted by people, traffic, or noise he wasn't used to. This became apparent when we watched a local rugby match. The game was between two teams from the same club. Amal and Paul, Allan's son from a previous marriage, played in opposition. The event was low-key, but there was still a lot of banter and shouting, all in playful fun. It seemed to disturb Ali. People standing close behind him made him uneasy. Loud bursts of laughter or people shouting encouragement to the players made him cringe. When Ali used to play and support his Rugby team all those years ago in Oxford, he was as vociferous as anyone else.

I asked, "Are you enjoying it? Does it bring back memories?"

He shook his head sideways to indicate no and mumbled, "Yes, I can remember."

His distress became worse in the crowded clubhouse after the game was over. Before, Ali would have brushed off accidental contact had not batted an eyelid. He was different now. He held his hands before him, palms outstretched, ensuring nobody entered his personal space.

Concerned, I whispered in his ear, "Are you okay?"

He shook visibly, pleading, "Please, can we go?"

I told the others we needed to get out fast by moving a finger across my throat, indicating 'cut', without Ali seeing.

They all understood. Allan immediately asked Ali, "Do you want to go?" Ali nodded yes.

That night, Ali was subdued and wanted to go to bed early. Once in bed, he said nothing other than, "Night."

After that experience, we avoided crowded places. We ensured that there would just be our small family group if we went out anywhere. One of the James children said, "There's a New Year's Day swim at Saundersfoot Beach; who's up for it?"

I looked to check Ali's response, unsure if he was listening, so I answered for both of us, "Please go. Don't worry about us."

To my surprise, Ali butted in, "I would love to go."

Amina, knowingly looking at me for support, said, "There will be loads of people going."

Ali knowingly replied, "I will be fine."

Unsure it was a good idea, I asked Ali again, "You sure?"

"Sure, I need some fresh air."

We parked some distance away from the main crowd of completely bonkers swimmers. Ali and I watched as our little group chased the main crowd into the freezing sea, some squealing, some diving into the waves in an act of bravado.

During the interlude, while the others were engaged in their daring exploit, we had time to talk. "Ali, are you okay? Please tell me what bothers you."

"I wish I knew. I think it's people's reaction to me. When they are close, I feel out of control of my emotions."

"Do you mean you feel threatened by them?"

"Maybe, but it's more than that."

"Go on."

"When they look at me, I see pity in their eyes."

"But you look away on purpose; you don't engage with strangers."

"That's because I don't want their pity."

"Ali, you look different now, but strangers don't know that, do they."

"Why do they avoid me then?"

"Ali, it's the other way around."

"I don't want to be like this."

"I know you will get better. It will take some time."

The freezing swimmers surrounded us, demanding towels and hot toddies, exclaiming how wonderful and exhilarating it was diving into the icy sea.

Smiling and almost flashing his new white dentures, Ali said, "Next year, count me in."

Through chattering teeth, Allan replied, "Deal."

Ali retorted, "There's only one real swimmer here. Perhaps she will make a promise, too."

"If you mean me, look away. No chance unless it's 25 degrees centigrade or more." The gang called me a wuss in unison. "I think you mean wise." This caused more funny remarks aimed at me.

Chapter 23
Back at Frimley Hospital

Ali seemed more at ease with himself once back in the environment he had become accustomed to. To be fair to him, he was trying to regain his fitness, but progress was slow. Visiting times were restricted, and we had little to discuss besides his slow progress. Other than seeing Ali, I had very little to occupy my mind. I remained at my father's flat, but he wasn't much company as he became consumed with finding Fatima. Amnesty International warned him several times that digging too much might compromise his safety. As a network of loyalist Syrians worked in London, he had to be careful not to fall into the trap of asking the wrong person. Even though he had installed a virtual private network onto his computer, which hid his location, I wasn't sure if that was enough and insisted he be careful. There were forums and groups of people like him trying to trace their lost ones on the internet. Luckily, my father was intelligent enough to realise that posting anything online might lead to him giving himself away. So, he just read postings, which further distressed him as so many others were in the same situation, intensifying that the task was hopeless.

George stayed connected and continued visiting Ali, but we never met other than accidentally. George was single again. I am unsure who ended his relationship with Hua. *Would he ever settle down?*

The weeks rolled into months, and nothing really happened. I applied for a position at Amnesty International, and the interview went well. After extensive positive background checks, I was told that a job would be offered soon.

Ali's health took an unexpected dive. I thought maybe he had caught a cold or had the flu. Blood tests proved that he had immunodeficiency. I was unsure what this meant, so I requested an appointment with Mr Phillips. He told me his immune system was attacking his body, one of the side effects of his medication. I was confused about why this disease attacked him now. So, I questioned Mr. Phillips, who responded, "I don't know, honestly."

"Do you mean the drugs you gave him could cause this?"

"Unfortunately, the answer is yes, but caused is the wrong word; facilitated is better."

"So, why did you give them to him."

"Because there is nothing else, it's difficult to establish what triggers the attack."

"So, you gave him a drug and weren't sure of it, is that correct?"

"You could say that, but only five drugs are available to us, and they target different triggers."

"So you just pick one at random?"

"Not exactly; from our growing database, we can usually break it down to one or two, sometimes three."

"I remember you told me you changed his drugs when he had an episode, so he is now on the second drug, yes?"

"That's correct; we will try another drug now."

"When will you know if the third one is correct?"

"It should take a few months; I must ascertain the correct drug, but the dosage is also important."

"When will you know for sure?"

"We take blood samples at regular intervals. They will be the indicator."

"So, you could kill him?"

"I wouldn't use those words, but we might be unable to save him."

"So, it's a gamble then?"

"There are other things in play. Some of it might be down to Ali himself."

"What do you mean? Are you saying he wants to die?"

"No, but how much fight does he have left?"

"Ali is a fighter. He will never give up; you don't know him."

"Sorry, but I must tell you he also has tuberculosis."

"Where did he get that from?"

"Not sure, possibly in prison."

"That was months ago. Why now?"

"Probably lying dormant until his immune system shut down."

"He is not going to die, not now, not after all the fighting he has done to stay alive, is he?"

"We will try our best; that's what we have been doing since he came here."

"So, he is going to get better then?"

"No promises. We will try everything at our disposal."

"Doctor, he has been through so much. Pull him through, please."

"While we have been talking, he has been transferred to the intensive care unit."

"Can I see him?"

"Later. Unfortunately, the visiting times are restricted, and only one person at a time, and you must be masked and gowned."

Chapter 24

Bad News

I didn't tell anyone how serious Ali's condition was, hoping I wouldn't have to. Not only was visiting restricted to me but the time spent with him was also limited.

Over the next few weeks, I told everyone that he was recovering slowly, which was not the reality but what I had hoped. That was until the day I was called into Mr Phillips' office for a consultation. It was a regular occurrence, so I entered his office. I expected to be greeted by the confident consultant informing me of Ali's progress.

Instead, a sombre face greeted me with, "Please take a seat, Mrs Mansour."

To begin with, I brushed off his demeanour as he had bad days before when he appeared impatient and frustrated. So, I just said, in a cheery voice, "Good morning," I hoped that would help swing his mood.

"Tea or coffee?"

"Coffee, please, black, no sugar." *He must have a bit of time on his hands.*

He sat back on his chair as though to put some distance between us before leaning forward, talking slowly and purposely. "There's no easy way of telling you this."

My stomach churned. Stunned, I asked, "How long?"

"Sorry, imminent."

"What does that mean?"

"He's going to be switched to palliative care today."

"What does that mean?"

"We are preparing a pathway to the end of life."

The words 'end of life' meant so little to me before. We all have one, but not Ali, not him. "How could that be?"

"His body has given up; we tried everything but failed."

Tears didn't come; I couldn't understand why.

"You're in shock. Is there anyone who can help you?"

"My father. I have friends, too."

"We have a priest, or pastor, whatever denomination, to help, if you want."

"No, I don't need anyone like that."

"Do you want us to contact your friends for you? We have all their details."

"No, I should do that; they should hear it from me, not a stranger."

"I know I was thinking of the time, that's all."

"Time?"

"Yes, it's imminent."

"Uh-oh, sorry, I will phone them now. For Christ's sake, you have only just told me."

"Do you need something, maybe a sedative?"

"No, thank you, I'll bloody well manage."

"Okay."

"Sorry, Doctor, I feel so angry. I want to smash something."

"It's to be expected. I'll arrange for a hospital car to take you home and give you some sedatives for tonight."

"Can I see Ali first?"

"Of course, take as much time as needed."

Ali looked no different; he was asleep and so peaceful I didn't wake him. I sat beside him like in Antalya, thinking it wasn't him. It hasn't been him since the Arab Spring; it wasn't me, either.

After telling Baba, who was shocked and could offer no more than fatherly hugs, I contacted the James household. Amina answered the phone, as always. It wasn't easy to tell them; the shock in their voices and the need for them to get answers wasn't helpful, so I was abrupt and to the point by saying Ali was dying.

When I phoned George, it was less complicated; I think he already knew, probably before me, so he listened and asked nothing of me. I sobbed, "Why, George, why the good people? Why not the evil bastards? Why, George, why?"

"Margaret, do you want me to come over? I have something that will help you sleep."

"I don't want to sleep; I want to remember Ali as he was. Good night, George."

Ali was hooked to various devices, his eyes closed, breathing lightly. He looked peaceful. All the friends Ali had in this world were sat waiting for him to die. Emre, my father, was in a nearby room. Amina, Allan, George, and I said goodbye and told him we loved him but were unsure if he could hear. Then, his life support was turned off.

I remembered what Ali told me when he was in a coma; he could hear and smell some things. So I wore his favourite perfume and ran my finger down his forehead onto his lips, hoping he would realise it was me. Allan and Amina held his hands, and George called him a wizard. Then we sat silently, not knowing when the life monitor would stop. When the beep-beep eventually stopped, proving he was no longer with us, I wondered if Ali heard the silence like we did. Did he think he was back on the same unknown journey in Raqqa prison, lying on the hamman floor, content that all the suffering and pain was over?

I was unsure if Ali could hear, so I sat quietly until the nurses came to ask if I needed anything. Then I did cry, not aloud but aching deep inside. I could hear the others sobbing as they stood beside my chair.

Ali's wishes were fulfilled; he entered the ocean on New Year's Day with the James family at Saundersfoot. Not all his ashes went into the sea. I saved some so my father could get closure, too. We sprinkled Ali's ashes amongst the gorse bushes at my mother's favourite place overlooking Barafundle Bay. To my father and I, it epitomised the grief of losing those we had loved. I remembered my mother, deep in thought, gazing at the ocean. Of Ali, when he was well, caring and loving, and when he was ill and wanted to visit this place with me. I assumed my father was remembering my mother and the death of Fatima, which he had now come to terms with.

Chapter 25

Life Without Ali

I am now working with Amnesty International; for some reason, I told my friends I worked for UNICEF. I am unsure why I told them that. Perhaps an air of secrecy, or because it was the start of a new life, my life without Ali.

I usually worked out of the head office in London. In London, I mostly stayed at my father's flat, which was ideal and very private. My father never got over the loss of Fatima, like I never got over the loss of Ali.

Ali's words, borrowed from George, 'live for today', had become my motto. Now, it meant something completely different than it did for Ali and me. Then, it was a bond that kept Ali and me together for as long as it lasted. It was just me; I didn't need anyone else, and no one would ever replace Ali.

There was one other person who realised that; George. I was exactly what George was looking for a mature woman with no strings attached. So, for a while, that's what 'living for today' looked like for George and me. Convenient for both of us.

I am not sure for what reason George changed. Maybe my lack of jealousy or commitment frustrated him.

Or perhaps he assumed I was behaving like him. When we were together for extended periods, he wanted to be with me all the time. To begin with, I thought it was another of George's ploys. So, I asked him, "Are you seeing anyone else?"

"No, are you?"

"No. Why aren't you playing the field? I don't mind."

"Doesn't appeal to me anymore."

"Why?"

"There's no point; we are such a good team."

"What if I were to play the field? Would that be okay, George?"

"That would break me."

"George, are you jealous?"

"You wouldn't, though, would you?"

"I might; why not?"

"Because I have never felt this way before."

"You tell all your conquests that."

"But this time, I mean it."

"George, you're like a broken record."

"You are not listening; this is different."

"George, can I give you some good advice?"

"Go on."

"Just live for today."

The End

Milton Keynes UK
Ingram Content Group UK Ltd.
UKHW010618291123
433416UK00001B/55